THE MANOR OF LEW

by

Cicely Briggs

Produced by Praxis Books, 1993.

ISBN 0-9518729-3-1

The author asserts the moral right to be identified as the author of this work.

Printed by Adprint, Pulborough, West Sussex, from artwork supplied.

Available from Mrs C.F. Briggs,
Little Goose, Lew Down, Okehampton,
Devon. EX20 4PU

Note: A few last-minute errors have been noted, as follows: bottom of p.15, second para. up. *Arthur* should read *Willy*. page 27, second paragraph from the bottom. The last sentence should read "With this idea goes that we do not have to be linked by apparent blood relationships in the present, but are linked by something far stronger...." page 61 – Cicely married in 1916, not 1917, and managed the house after her marriage.
Apologies from the Editor for typographical errors.

PREFIX

For a short span of our lives, we are allowed the custodianship of a tiny portion of the Earth's surface. How we treat that portion of the bounty of this Planet is indelibly recorded in the very structure of the evolution of life.

This booklet is an introspective view of the way this house has developed its general character, its vibrations, its structure. The legal owners have played a leading influence in the way it takes its own particular vibration or ray of individuality. But we must also remember that it is not ONLY the titular owners of these places, such as you and I with our own modest homes, but it is you and I who control the actual development of the ideas and give it the "feelings, the sensitivities". We give it the form which we in this day and age call "vibrations" in a very loose and unknowing way. Yet we all have at some stage stated that we have or have not "liked" the "feel" of a place. What created these feelings? We have to watch our actions, and refuse to earth any destructive thoughts: that is involution, not evolution! This creates the essence and atmosphere of the house.

THE OPENING OF THE EVENTS

William the Conqueror quite unwittingly created a precedent in 11th century England. His marauding armies spread like a plague of blood sucking vampires over Saxon England. They looted, stole, murdered, raped. William himself, the prime example of this type of conquering destroyer, annexed by force 176 Estates in Devonshire alone, at the same time liquidating the owners. Not content with these stolen acquisitions, he levied taxes against the Estate owners. He became famous for the first Estate Tax records. His decree was that any house of substance in the year 1086 should be put into the record book with the fullest details.

This book was originally called *Inquisto Gheldi*, and only later came to be called *The Doomsday Book* – an apt title for such a tax on those poor owners of these heavily laden possessions. It was also known as *The Book of Substance*. Today this is an interesting book of reference. There were sections and areas within each county, and the specific book for Devonshire was called *The Exeter Book of Records*, which contained many graphic details.

William's objective was purely mercenary. Historically he will be remembered for the first records, which are very interesting. They list the Estates and the names of the families in existence at the time. Dispossessions are recorded, and the names of the new owners who were given Estates for services rendered. Strangely, he is better remembered for his tax collection than for other achievements.

In those days the unit of measurement for an area was a "hundred". This was worked out by grouping a hundred families together. The term endured for some time, until, for obvious reasons, changes occured due to either the growth or the destruction of a community. Later in this booklet, I have quoted from a book of records known as the *Lifton Hundreds*. The House of Lew is of ancient origin; it is recorded as being in existence at the time of William I. The spelling has changed with the years and, presumably, from the whim of the current owner. It has been Leuya, Lewe, Lew, Lew Trenchard, Lewen House, Leure House and Ley House.

✧✧✧✧✧✧✧

LEW TRENCHARD

Quotation from *The Devonshire Doomsday Book*. Page 388:

INQUISTO GHELDI (being the taxation of the Hundreds) "*ROGERIUS de MOLES – tenet de Baldvino – LEWE – (LEUYA) which 'BRICTRIC' tenebat tempore Regis Edwardi et geldabat pro dimidia Hida – Terra –* " etc.

Translation: Roger de Moles of Baldwin with a manor "Held" called Leuya – which BRISTERIC held on the day on which King Edward was alive, and it rendered gold for half a Hide. Seven ploughs can plough this and now Roger de Moles holds it of Baldwin. There Roger had one plough in demesne and villeins six ploughs. Roger has twelve villein and eight Borders and six serfs and eighteen head of cattle, fifty sheep and thirty acres of meadow, sixty acres of pasture worth £4. But when Baldwin received it it was worth sixty shillings."

In 1086 the house was a Royal Manor, ranking as "Knights status with the order to provide three Horsemen for the Kind as this knights 'fee'."

Houses thus recorded had to be of some substance to be considered worth annexing, then taxing. Thus the Bristeric referred to as holding the Manor in King Edward's life must have been the local reigning Saxon Thane, who was dispossessed by the Conqueror when he acquired 178 Manor Houses in Devonshire at the time of the Conquest. He subsequently gave all of these to his cousin Baldwin, and made him Sheriff of Devon.

Baldwin, in his turn, leased Leure House to one of his relatives, Rogerius de Mole, with the land mentioned above, for which he paid the princely rent of £4. History does not record the length of his stay, for next we hear of the Trenchards owning this property, although Rogerius and his descendants are supposed to have held this "fee" (Manor) until the reign of Edward III, which was

The wood hewer – imagine an axe in place of the saw

in 1327. But there are records in Stowford (an adjoining parish) of the Trenchards before this date. The name means in effect "Les Trenchen", the wood hewer. We can only suppose that as this was a densely forested area, that these wood hewers were the "New Rich" of the time, and were thus in a position to upgrade themselves and purchase the local manor house when the de Mole family left. This is only supposition – I have found no records to this effect. The Trenchards, strangely, gave their names to the house and hamlet, yet appear to have been in residence as a family the shortest period.

The house then passed to the Monk family of Potheridge as the "apanage" of the second son sometime in 1556.

At the time of the Saxon Thane and William the Conqueror, there was a lake, the top of which was Gaulford, so named by the Romans, meaning *forked way*. This forked way referred to the road branching off to Lydford. There had been a notable battle when the Britons were repulsed and driven back over the Tamar; at this point the farm is called "Slaughter". Not half a mile from here, below Point (bridge), the Lake "Loch in Looe" extended well over three miles to the old Coryton Station. It discharged into the River Lydd, the evidence of this is visible to us now by the deposits it has left on the banks fo the farmland so close to Lew House. On the East Side, near the farms of Wooda and Galford are relics of early civilisations comprising flint and early bronze age artifacts, also a Roman encampment.

At that time the original Manor House of the Ruling Thane is thought to have been where the Mill and Dower House now stand. These buildings were on a spit of land running out into this Lake, this seems likely as water was an essential tool harnessed for power.

The Big House must have been moved further along the valley on the higher ground sometime during Edward III's reign, for coins of this period have been found in the walls of the house. The present Mill House and farm with Dower House are very old buildings though sadly reduced in size. The Mill is now non-active with no water left to work the wheels.

Sabine Baring-Gould always felt that the present Dower House was in fact the site of the original Manor House of Leuya.

THE MONK FAMILY

As already stated, the Monks purchased Leuya Manor from the Trenchards, some say through marriage, in 1556.

Sir Thomas Monk fell into debt in 1623 and found himself in Exeter Gaol. His second son was the famous George Monk, who should have inherited Leuya House if his father had not been forced to sell. Henry Gould was related by the marriage of his daughter Mary to Thomas Monk's other son. We can only assume that some family arrangement was made by Henry Gould, who was the Mortgagee, to purchase the house from Thomas Monk Senior. In 1626, the first Gould purchased Lew.

George Monk, 1st Duke of Albemarle, a famous General and Admiral of the Fleet, was first a Parliamentary soldier, who then became a Royalist. It was due to his efforts, and those of his uncle James Gould, Mayor of Exeter, that King Charles II was returned to the throne after Cromwell's death. In fact, as Admiral of the Fleet he went in person to escort the King back to England. For this, the grateful Charles gave George the dukedom of Albemarle, thus amply compensating him for the loss of Lew House as a second son's inheritance lost through debt. His portrait is in the Gallery at Lew.

Sir Thomas Monk

HENRY GOULD

Henry married Ann, and their initials are seen carved in the overmantle in the front hall. This was a present to commemorate their wedding and the acquisition of Lew House. Henry had other large properties but lived chiefly at Floyers Hayes in Exeter. He was an affluent banker, who only used Lew House as a residence when administering the estate, for collecting rents and so on. But, after his death, his widow Ann finished her days at the Dower House of Lew, the old original house.

Henry had two brothers, Nicholas, who became a baronet, and the famous James Gould who was Mayor of Exeter in 1648 and High Sheriff of the County of Devon.

JAMES GOULD

James was a highly colourful personality. What he lacked in stature he most certainly made up for in courage and loyalty, for he was an ardent Royalist. He consistently refused to acknowledge the Cromwellian administration, and was fined £200 for refusing to accept some of the new Cromwellian ministers. One of his acts of defiance was to purchase the lead and the great bells of Exeter Cathedral, saving them from the threat of Puritan vandalism.

James and his nephew George Monk were responsible for the return of Charles II. Unfortunately James died before the King was restored to the throne, but his loyalty was rewarded as a member of his family, Nicholas Gould, was knighted by Charles II.

EDWARD and JAMES GOULD

Edward and James,. the sons of James the Mayor, were wealthy men in their own rights, both being successful merchantmen. James was a "China merchant", and on one of his trips to China he had a model in clay made of himself dressed as a Mandarin, as a joke for his wife. This still remains in the house. Portraits of both these prosperous merchants hang in the Front Hall.

COLONEL WILLIAM GOULD

During Cromwell's time, the Gould family, like many others of that period, became divided. Whilst James was expressing his loyalties as a Royalist, his cousin William Gould was fighting for Cromwell. In fact William became famous for the battles which he commanded in and around Plymouth — Mount Gold was originally called Mount Gould after his successful siege. His portrait also hangs in the Front Hall.

The relics of these divided days are the remaining hidden passages, most of which have now been blocked off or absorbed into the new house. There are persistent rumours of tunnels from the house to a farm some miles away which purport to cross beneath the present A30 road. The farm in question was part of the estate, but in another parish.

Lt-Gen CHURCHILL

Lt-Gen Churchill was brother to the Duke of Marlborough and married the daughter of James Gould of Dorchester. There is a portrait of John Churchill and his mother Sarah in the Ballroom of the house. The Churchills lived in Dorset at that time as a comparitively humble farming family. It was only upon the rise to fame of John Churchill in the reign of Queen Anne that the name was raised from the ranks of obscurity.

EDWIN THORATON GOULD

Edwin was the great grand nephew of Mayor Henry Gould. He was left huge sums of money by his grand uncles Edward and James, the two merchantmen. He married Lady B. Yelverton. Despite the wealth that he inherited, and marrying wealth, he was a wastrel and a spender; he ended his days in banishment for debt in France. His son became Baron de Ruthven through his mother's inheritance.

CAPTAIN EDWARD GOULD

Another gambler and rogue was yet another Edward Gould, referred to as "The Scamp". His father, William Drake Gould, inherited several estates through his uncles, including Lew Trenchard, but he preferred to live at Pridhamsleigh, near Staverton, Ashburton. William had married a very interesting and famous character known as Margaret Belfield, who was eight years his senior. They had two children, Edward and Margaret. William died when he was in his forties, and Edward, "The Scamp" inherited four estates. The poor Scamp has been held up to the family as the black sheep or skeleton in the cupboard. He was, for a short time, a Captain in the Army, and was reputed to be short-tempered, sadistic, weak and a compulsive gambler. How much of this has been embellished through time is guesswork. He certainly gambled away all his estates, bar Lew Trenchard, which he mortgaged for ninety years to his mother Margaret Belfield Gould — known affectionately as "Madam".

Unfortunately for Edward, he became involved with an unscrupulous but clever young relative by the name of John Dunning, who was a brilliant but ambitious barrister and lawyer, and a far better card player than Edward. He

Lady Ashburton – Elizabeth

eventually won all the Estates from the Goulds, became 1st Lord of Ashburton, and died shortly after marrying Elizabeth Gould, leaving an infant son. Lady Ashburton long outlived her boorish and ugly husband. There is a particularly beautiful portrait of her at Lew. Her son became the 2nd Lord Ashburton, but the title died out soon after.

Edward became involved in a murder charge; he had been gambling and had as usual lost heavily. Later that evening he rode off, dressed as a Highwayman, held up his gambling partner and shot him. There was a witness who claimed it was moonlight and that he saw "The Scamp"'s face after he had shot his victim.

John Dunning defended Edward and won the case, claiming that the witness could not have identified Edward as it was not moonlight. He produced a calendar with the dates and phases altered by him. In those days, almanacs were limited in number, and only a few people has access to them. But it seems strange to us now that such a simple alteration was not checked. But John Dunning succeeded in getting Edward acquitted. This trial was very expensive and helped bring about the final ruin. In 1777 Edward was penniless, and he died a few years later.

The only request he made was to be buried in Bath Abbey beside the lady he loved. She had been forcibly married to a third party, but she and Edward ran away together. How she died, or when, history does not relate, but it seems that to Edward she was the only thing that mattered. Again it is not known whether his request to be buried beside her was granted.

MARGARET – "Old Madam"

Margaret saved Lew Trenchard. She was an astute, dominant personality and managed the estates with great ability. By the time she died, at the age of 90 in 1795, she had substantially increased and improved the entire property. There are many stories (one of them is told in Sabine Baring-Gould's *A Book of Folklore)* that she continues to walk the estates and walk the house. Perhaps she feels that she still has to administer. These rumours of her visitations persist, although facts are hard to establish. Let us hope that she is now at peace, for she worked hard and persistently for the increase and prosperity of her home.

WILLIAM BARING-GOULD

William was the grandson of Margaret and William Gould of Lew Trenchard.

One day, we might have found him out walking through the woods on his beautiful Courtlands estate near Exeter, which had been left to him by his banker father, Charles Baring. He walked through the sunlit woods, the ground heavily covered with wood anemones underfoot. He had come out here to make a decision.

Margaret Belfield (Young "Madam")

His grandmother had willed that if he were to inherit Lew Trenchard property, he was to add the name of Gould, making the surname into *Baring-Gould*. He had no love for Lew Trenchard, which he had visited many times. He had no enthusiasm for his grandmother's idea. He and his family evidently lived a high social life, and the incredibly rural and isolated position of Lew House, nearly forty miles from Exeter and his social activities did not appeal to him.

History tells us that it was lack of finance which won the day. William took on the full name, and the estate that he disliked. His feelings coloured his whole approach to the way he became custodian of Lew estate, and he took little interest in any part of it.

He had none of his father's business acumen. As a banker, Charles had become immensely rich and his family lacked for nothing. His son, like all rich men's sons, could spend easily, yet he was always short of money. The home at Courtlands that he loved was huge and pretentious, and he lived a sophisticated social life. He was a popular fellow, a good-looking, kind-hearted man, nicknamed "The Adonis of Devon" for his looks. He was the father of six marriageable children, four daughters and two sons. Three of his daughters (the fourth was unlucky enough to have a hare lip) were considered to be the most startling beauties

William Baring (Gould). The Adonis of Devon

of their day. When they were seen "abroad", walking or riding in their carriages, particularly on one occasion in Italy, following Lord Nelson's triumphant journey, they caused a considerable commotion when everyone rushed out to see these famous lovelies.

Amelia Sabine, their mother, was herself considered good looking, despite her temper. She came from a good family, and the marriage brought the names of Sabine and Baring together. The whole family were blond, slender and with the most startling blue eyes. Sabine himself inherited these looks and passed them to his children.

William arranged a good marriage for his son Edward, and all his children eventually married well. Edward, the "Silver Poplar" had a very lavish socialite wedding in Exeter. Both William's sons bought commissions in the Indian Army.

Amelia hated the enforced move to Lew Trenchard as much as William did. They never came to terms with it and it seems likely that their attitude passed to Edward, their son. William remained insolvent and was forever trying to raise money. We have a letter in which he asks Edward to help him out financially, but we don't know whether the money was forthcoming.

William's other son, William Drake, went into the army and served in India. His memorial stone is in Lew Trenchard Church, suggesting that the "wrong" son inherited the Estate. There is a mystery surrounding his death, which happened at the early age of 33 in Quetta, Baluchistan (Northern India at the time). It was reported that he died of fever, but there are persistent rumours that he was murdered for his attentions to a lady of his heart. He was married, but little is known of the precise circumstances. By chance I was sent a copy of one of the last letters he must have written to his mother, Amelia. Unfortunately, the cost of postage was so high relative to their army pay, the habit was to write across the letter in both directions, making it difficult to read. I have a photostat of this letter. The original must have been sold sometime in 1931 when the house was empty and much was sold, looted or pinched in lieu of salaries owed to the existing caretaker staff.

William drifted into Lew Trenchard bringing in many changes, altering and introducing a new and very interesting name within the family, adding Baring to Gould, but also introducing the name of Sabine to the family christian names. He also altered the church, renewing its furnishings and removing much of the old contents. His efforts were not to Sabine's taste.

There are at present at least three Sabines in this scattered family, and the name holds to this day.

William died at Lew, and his gravestone is in the churchyard.

AMELIA SABINE

She came from the famous Sabine family. Her father, Jospeh Sabine of Tewin, Herts, later became Lt. Gen. Sabine, Governor General of Gibraltar. The portraits of him and his wife are in the Ballroom. Amelia herself was a herbalist, and she administered her own homemade potions to the estate workers. An indomitable lady with a rather viperish tongue, William was considered to be a saint being married to her.

SIR EDWARD SABINE

Amelia's brother Edward was an Arctic explorer who became engaged to an American lady prior to his Arctic journey. They swore fidelity and love, she promising to await his return. Alas, his journey took three years, and in the meantime his fiancée, wearied of the long wait, had found another. By the time Edward returned, his lady was married and the mother of a daughter.

Sir Edward, an astute and tough man, swore to her that he would return when the baby reached the age of fourteen and again ask for her hand in marriage. Much to the lady's disgust, despite the fact that she was now a widow, fourteen years later, Sir Edward did return, and married the daughter. A strange situation, as the poor young bride had to take her mother into her home, since Sir Edward insisted she needed schooling in housekeeping ways.

Although the child bride was so young, she could write and speak several languages. She was reputed to be very plain, but she had a powerful sense of humour. She wrote a journal and it is from her own writings that we hear of the hours she had to sit translating dreary classics for her husband, or acting as an intermediary between her mother and her husband in their eternal bickerings. Fortunately, so great was her sense of humour that she seems to have made light of her strange domestic life. Sir Edward lived to a ripe old age, his wife predeceasing him.

Sir Edward Sabine

Sir Edward was an ornithologist of some renown. There is a "Sabine Gull" — presumably named by him.

SUSANNAH GOULD

Another poignant marriage was that of Susannah, who was the aunt of William Drake Gould. She is supposed to haunt the house dressed in white and is referred to as "The Virgin bride". She fell in love with Peter Truscott, whose father John Truscott was given "the living" of the church by Henry Gould. Unfortunately, Henry and John were at loggerheads politically and over their respective religious beliefs. There appears to have been only one occasion when these two were united in thought, and that was when they discovered that their respective children wished to marry; then they were mutually determined to prevent the marriage.

Despite the feud, Susannah married her Peter in Lew Trenchard Church, but alas, as she walked back to the house, she dropped dead, supposedly from a heart attack. She was buried two days after her wedding, on March 21st 1729.

The ghost of Susannah

It is my belief that a girl with the spirit to thwart her family and marry her man would not die of the vapours so young. I believe that she haunts the house trying to tell us that she was poisoned. (There are many poisons which induce symptoms resembling heart failure). Or maybe she is just looking for her Peter. He remained faithful to her memory and never married again. He lived on in the parish until his own death.

Peter's father planted the lime trees in the churchyard as an emblem of his beliefs as a Whig. Henry planted the fir trees as an emblem of his Jacobite beliefs. They appear to have fought on to the death.

THE SILVER POPLAR - EDWARD BARING-GOULD

Edward Baring-Gould was nicknamed "The Silver Poplar" by his wife Sophie and her family for his tall slender good looks and his blond hair. There is a portrait of him in his pale blue uniform of the Madras Light Cavalry in the service of the East India Company. It shows a very handsome figure of a man. The uniform has been given to the National Army Museum. It is at present with the Royal Military Academy, Sandhurst. It can be viewed, if prior warning is given to Mrs Hopkins, Head of the Department of Uniform, Badges and Medals.

Edward was the eldest son of William Baring-Gould and Amelia Sabine (Baring-Gould). He inherited Lew House on the death of his father in 1846. It was a property he had little liking for.

He married Sophie Charlotte, the daughter of Admiral Bond, who lived in Exeter.

The story goes that he was out in his carriage or gig, and the wheel came off in the ruts. The gig turned on its side and his companion — a man of considerable girth — fell on top of him, dislocating his hip. I have a feeling that they were probably racing the gig, testing the horse's paces, over very rough ground, when disaster hit them. It was evidently a terrible blow for Edward, and he remained restless ever after, finding it impossible to live in rural England, especially a "backwoodsey place like Lew Down".

He started his married life with the long suffering and very fine personality, Sophie. For fifteen years he dragged her and her increasing family around Europe. The order of the travelling packages would be something like this: first their silver, their baggage, their children and their two or three retainers, travelling endlessly to whatever places took Edward's fancy.

Edward Baring-Gould

He was a great reader, so he had to choose places where the mail could arrive without delay and ensure that he could read the latest Dickens novel or any other literature of the day.

Unlike his amiable much-loved father, Edward was a man of steel. If he made up his mind on a subject, there was no arguing or interfering. He was excessively hard on his children. He believed that children's minds were like sponges, absorbing material put into it, regardless of the aptitude of the child. He evidently had great yearnings to have been an engineer, so insisted that his three sons should learn maths, that they could become engineers in his place. He had them coached, chivvied and chased to the right tutors to receive the required coaching. Only one became an engineer, but he (we believe) had a nervous breakdown as a result. Sabine, made of sterner material, just failed hopelessly in that department. His coaches had to admit defeat, and even to his dying day, Sabine could not work out the simplest mathematics. He used to take his sums to the kitchen staff for them to work it out for him.

In Sabine's *Book of Reminiscences* he refers to letters from his mother when they were abroad, in which she speaks very fondly of her husband's conciliatory way with her. She too must have been made of sterner stuff, since he was as insensitive as she was sensitive. Never a complaint from her, he went his dogmatic Victorian ways. His children scratched an education wherever they happened to spend a winter or spring. They managed to become bilingual, or in Sabine's case, he learned about eight languages. He could teach himself a new language from a dictionary, and did so in the case of Icelandic. Unwittingly, Edward produced a very literary son. His other two sons were not so fortunate.

Eventually, after some fifteen years of wandering, Edward brought his family back to live in Devonshire. In the meantime, the house had been leased to all and sundry, with caretakers in charge who were paid a bare pittance. Thus, it was in a bad state of repair. It is believed that the family lived in Bratton Clovelly, for a period, perhaps while the house was being cleaned up.

He seems to have been short of money, for he started mining projects in the location of the house. Many of these foundered early on. He made many tools himself, both for mining and for agriculture. He wanted to try out new tools to work the land, but he had little success. The local tenant farmers preferred their age-old methods to his newfangled implements which were forever breaking down.

When Sabine inherited the estate and his young family moved into it, Mary wrote a letter in which she referred to the mess of broken tools littering the estate, testimony to many past failures.

For all of Edward's hardness and rigidity, he seemed to have a way of finding devoted wives. Sophie Charlotte died in 1863, leaving four children: Sabine, Margaret, William and Edward Drake. Edward then married Lavinia Snow. She was much younger than Edward and survived him for some time. She died in 1922, leaving two children by Edward as well as two by her first husband, a Mr Marshall.

Edward died in 1872. he had to relent towards his eldest son, who demanded to go into the church. None of his sons followed the professions he chose for them. This must have been a bitter pill.

Sophie Charlotte Baring-Gould and Sabine Baring-Gould, circa 1840.

SOPHIE CHARLOTTE

She was the daughter of Admiral Bond and married Edward Baring-Gould in 1832. She must have been very good looking, and according to her son, Sabine, who was devoted to her, she had a very gentle personality and strong Christian principles. She hated gossip of any sort and hated the terrible poverty she witnessed in her travels, and actively played the part of Lady Bountiful, bringing food to the tables of those who had not eaten. One of her best-known sayings is "Put all your thoughts and comments through three sieves – is it first true? is it kind? and is it just? If it does not measure up to these, do not say it." Sabine said that she had a spiritual sensitivity which was so strongly marked it was like a delicate nervous network enveloping her mind and soul, and which shrank as if with real pain from anything evil or unlovely.

She must have suffered intensely in the fifteen years travelling enforced by her harsh and restless spouse. She endured terrible travel sickness, and nearly died from lack of air every time she travelled by sea or coach. In some instances she had to be strapped to the deck of the ship.

After fifteen years, she was allowed to return and stay at peace at Lew, but unfortunately she died in 1863 from cancer of the jaw. This was thought to have been brought on by her false teeth which were made of rhino horns. There is a magnificent picture of her with Sabine as a small boy at the top of the main staircase.

LAVINIA SNOW

Lavinia Snow Maitland Marshall was a widow when she met Edward Baring-Gould. She had two Marshall children. She was tiny of stature – there is a picture of her with her son Lionel in which she looks very bent and frail. Lionel was a wonderful son to her, although he worked most of his life in America as a busy doctor and father of five children. Throughout the years of separation from her he wrote weekly letters to keep in touch. When funds permitted, he came over to visit her.

She evidently met her second husband through her brother, a great friend of Sabine, who became her stepson. She was almost Sabine's age – much younger than Edward, the "Silver Poplar". Despite his reputation as a hard insensitive father, it seems that his wives released something softer in his nature. Harsh treatment was the Victorian way with children, set by the behaviour of the Queen and her consort Albert. Lavinia was married to Edward for six or seven years and had two children by him.

She was greatly loved by her step-family. Some of them were almost her own age, and some were still very young. They referred to her as "Granny Ardoch". At her death the children of Lew Down made posies of flowers and placed them on her grave as a mark of their great respect for her. Most of her grandchildren through her son Lionel now live in the United States.

ARTHUR and LEILA

Lavinia and Edward's children were Arthur and Leila. Arthur went into the church and for a short time worked for his half-brother Sabine. There cannot have been enough work for two energetic Baring-Gould on one small place with few parishioners, so Arthur moved on. He worked in Brixham and Princetown before settling in Haverfordwest, in Pembrokeshire. This was a tough assignment and he remained there until his death. The parish was poverty-stricken and very run down, but Arthur built it up enormously and his name lives on in the locality. A hospital ward is named for him, and there are both a "Baring-Gould Way" and a "Baring-Gould Close" in the area.

Sabine and Arthur were very close, and Sabine was annoyed with the Exeter Diocese for letting such an able man slip from their midst.

Arthur had three children. Cedric, his son, lives in West Sussex and has two children; Irene (Widdicombe) is at the time of writing full of zest and vigour in her 90s; and Dora, whose family lives in the States. Irene adored Uncle Sabine and Aunt Grace and knew them well. She has written a memoir for this booklet (see page 45). I gather that Sabine, devoted to his step-mother, played joked on her. The following one caused much consternation, but was funny: apparently at the height of the war, Sabine went to the Post Office and sent off a telegram to Lavinia enclosing information as to the "call up" of her fat pony. The animal was to enlist immediately to help the war effort. There was considerable confusion until the hoax was discovered.

Sabine and Lavinia were friends into old age. He seems to have visited her frequently, and no doubt played many similar pranks on her over the years. She must have listened to his problems, and treated him with sympathy and kindness after Grace died.

Lavina's daughter Leila married Frank Carver and had two sons and a daughter. Jack had a daughter Leise (known to all as Flora), who is married and living in the Isle of Wight with her husband Alec.

This second branch of the Baring-Gould family is now quite a large group in its own right.

Lavinia apparently did not wish to live in the established Dower House, and decided on a hilltop house in the village of Lew Down. It boasted a fine view of Brentor Church on its hill, and was renamed "Ardoch Lodge", because in her childhood days she knew happy times in Scotland in a house of that name.

I understand that some children in the present newly-built house have felt Lavinia's presence. She seems to be still looking after the children of Lew Down. The huge central fireplace in the middle of the building is a reminder of its early days, as the framework, made of local stone, still remains.

MARGARET, WILLIAM (WILLY) AND EDWARD

These are Sabine's brothers and sister, of which we know little. Edward died at the age of thirty-seven, having been very weakened by being in a shipwreck. William, known as Willy by some, was a jolly and engaging child, according to his mother. Sabine quotes a letter in his *Early Reminiscences* to this effect. He was born in Bratton Clovelly in 1837. It was Willy who came closest to fulfilling his father's ambition that at least one of his sons should be an engineer. William worked on building a bridge somewhere in the United States, but had a mental breakdown. It is assumed that this was the result of the enormous pressures of his training and his father's relentless insensitivity. He seems to have taken after his grandfather, William Baring, known for his good looks and gentle ways, and nicknamed "The Adonis of Devon".

When he recovered from his breakdown, Willy enjoyed the rural life at the family home. There are hints of scandal in stories about him. Sabine had to guarantee to look after him, and on one occasion was called back to Devon to sort out something to do with rumours of riotous escapades at Lew House, which was at the time tenanted by a lively and curvaceous lady married to an elderly man. There is, indeed, some badly-hidden evidence that one of the Baring-Goulds was involved.

There are also constant claims around the area today of some unrecognised descendants of the Baring-Gould family, whose paternity is not proven. There is, however, a striking likeness of feature and character. Many of them have jolly personalities and striking good looks. Perhaps Willy did leave his mark behind; his spirit may have had a severe jolt under his father's domination, but he seems to have survived.

It must have been hard for Arthur following in Sabine's footsteps. They seem to have been very different in character. Sabine was a veritable tornado of energy, and Willy was easygoing and life-loving.

Margaret married a Rev. Theodore Henry Marsh, rector of Cawston in Norfolk. We have no record of any children.

SABINE BARING-GOULD. The Person

I must state at the very beginning that I never met my grandfather. He died while we were on our way back from India in 1924.

All my information is based on the words I have heard from those who did know him and from the information I have read of his life. It must be remembered that there were twelve surviving children who knew him intimately and some of them had children of my age and more. I have formed my impressions of him as a man dedicated to the work of God. However, as a family man he was an enigma – really difficult to understand. His whole character was complex, light and shade, likeable and very unlikeable; sensitive and totally insensitive. He attracted enormous respect, devotion and in many cases, love from his fellows and from some of his large family. But he was such a mixture. He showed, as many Victorians of his day appeared to do with their families, a complete autocracy. Their word in the home was Law, and the families had to jump at his word. It can only be assumed that such was the tone of the day, to show your family anything but discipline could be read as being detrimental to the welfare of the child. He had little to base his behaviour to his children on; the example of his own father perhaps gave him the "blueprint" for a Victorian father and husband. It is hard to equate the two sides of the man: his deep compassion for others, his loving care for the underdog and concern for the poor everywhere on the one hand and his tyranny in his own home on the other.

It would be totally erroneous of us in this liberal age to stand in judgement. Sabine certainly ran a totalitarian state in his home, and elicited fear from all but his wife. He behaved roughly towards his sons in particular. Grace alone could control him up to a point, with his work and his attitude towards the hierarchy of the church. She repeatedly calmed him when his anger rose at any form of hypocrisy. But she never managed to get him to sense her own frustrations and her own loneliness. She was a wife who was expected to fit into his life, regardless of her own feelings.

My mother had a bad accident when she was about ten years old. Sabine had instructed his children that none of them were to go up on the roof, where the men were working on the big bell on the chimney. Needless to say, children of all ages dodge authority if their curiosity is aroused. They all went up to investigate (the children tended to fall into groups of about five, according to their ages). My mother fell through the hole in the scaffolding and crashed onto her legs, severely damaging her

Sabine at about 30

feet. She was also knocked unconscious. Her brothers and sisters, rather than face up to their father's fury, carried her up to the avenue and were in the process of burying her when she recovered in the nick of time. She managed at morning and evening prayers not to show her limp, as the others crowded around her as she came into the room. But her feet were completely misshapen for the rest of her life. I tell this story to illustrate the degree the degree of discipline. Yet I wonder what he would have done, had he been told that they thought she was dead?

Sabine had a deeply volatile emotional body, which would change quickly from a plus to a minus in shades. He was given to great intolerance and it was hard to get him to change his mind. This could have been an inheritance from his own father, who also would not change his mind, though Sabine was much more tolerant than his parent.

Yet there are so many stories of his incredible compassion towards any who needed help. One example is the story of finding a parishioner at Christmas time with a household of children and no food or firewood. He went straight back to his house and ordered that this be remedied without delay.

Another story, with great humour: as he loved the unusual and was always willing to carry out any request asked of him. On this occasion he received an urgent summons to call in to see one of the poor old widows living in his parish. He arrived, to be met by the distraught lady wringing her hands.

"Maister, Oh Maister, me ole pig, 'er be a dying of, will 'ee do me a great favour, please to give her the last rites at once for 'er time is near." He obliged, and did not think her request anything out of the ordinary. The story goes that the pig rolled over and died after being released.

I have heard tales from some of his older grandchildren, that he was a wonderful storyteller, and would come up at bedtime to tell them some exciting tale, then bend and kiss them goodnight.

Joyce tells of the time when she and her sister stayed at Lew when their mother worked with the woman's army during the 1914-18 War. On one of these evening visits, he went as usual to the children's room, where they excitedly decided to tie up his rather long fair hair which grew to his shoulders. They very methodically tied it up, all bedecked with pale blue ribbons and made him promise not to take them out before morning. That evening someone called on him, and being reminded of his unusual hairstyle, he refused to break his promise, entertaining his visitor with a special hairstyle for the evening.

Another story from Joyce: she went out with him on his rounds in his gig with Charlie Dunstan handling the reins. Joyce was a chatty child and kept up an endless series of questions. She was sharply warned to keep her mouth still or she would be out of the gig. She must have been about six or seven at the time. She did not stop her flow, so Sabine ordered Charlie to stop the pony and put the child out on the road, then ordered him to drive on. Charlie became alarmed when they continued for some way, leaving the lonely child far behind, out of sight. He protested (Charlie often dared to challenge the Maister, as he was called). In some surprise, Sabine remembered what had happened. It had quite gone out of his mind.

He was habitually so full of ideas, several at a time, that he was given to cutting corners and not researching detail too deeply. He was sometimes judged on the resulting inaccuracies in his work, but detail to him was too time-consuming.

Over and over, I have heard of the love he generated from his grandchildren, at all ages. He had an amazing way of communicating with children and could be a child with them. It was sad that he was not like this with his own offspring. Presumably, the large number pressured him to provide food and clothes and schooling. He wanted to spend his time entirely on research and God's work. He was profoundly and deeply religious in the true sense – a man of God.

His whole face would glow with rapture when he was filled with thoughts of his Creator. Many said that his face took on a most beautiful expression on these occasions.

One cannot but admire his tremendous energy. Journeys anywhere took so much discomfort and time, either riding horseback or in a gig, or sometimes by train. He did everything with deep concentration and inner drive, taking in every detail. He enjoyed the experiences he had with his many men friends who had similar interests to his. One such was Mr Radford from Lydford. Sabine talks of the hospitality he received, and how welcome a hot meal was after a full day on the moors. Then he would ride the seven miles home, his mind seething with the information gleaned.

Sabine had almost superhuman energy and could outwork most people. He did most of his writing at night, standing at his high desk in the bedroom over the kitchens, so that he could be warm when all the world was sleeping around him.

His most mellow moments were those early hours in the morning when others were waking and starting the day. If he had finished a book or a chapter, all written in his small neat personal handwriting by flickering light, he would be brought a steaming cup of cocoa (his favourite drink) by a member of his family and they would ask his agreement to some favour they needed. They were quick enough to know that they had to act fast, before his mood turned. If it was to purchase a new horse, it meant going at once, at the crack of dawn, to buy it without delay. My mother tells of many such events when she would be off to Launceston to change her horse.

Sabine's eyesight was very poor. It had been damaged by the snows of Iceland, and the long hours of lamp-lit writing must have done further harm. No wonder (as the fable goes) he failed to recognise his own children at times!

He had a strange relationship with his sons, which may have been the shade of his own childhood casting its influence. He himself had had many severe beatings, and it is certain that his own sons had a hard time. They were sent to schools at first locally, in Tavistock. They had only one horse between them, so they rode and walked by turns. At the age of sixteen or so, he flung them out and told them to earn their own living. They were "landed gentry" and should not soil their hands, but they were expected to find work somehow. Two left England for the States, as a land of plentiful opportunities. They were given the steerage money to get to America and nothing more.

Sabine developed a great unreasoning dislike of America and things American. This may have to do with the fact that his emigrant sons did make their way successfully. Harry was not so fortunate. He worked as a navvy in Bristol docks and became mortally ill. A friend of his walked him back home from Bristol, to remain on the danger list for nearly six months. Then Sabine told him to get out and earn his living. He took a job in Borneo and was dead within a few months.

Yet Sabine was kindness itself to his parishioners if they were in trouble. There are many stories of his giving food to those without, ensuring they were housed and putting himself out in many personal ways.

He hardly noticed most of his daughters, but deeply loved Mary, his firstborn, and tolerated Daisy, a gifted artist. He would listen to Joan. So long as they kept out of his way, all went well. He was amazed when anyone congratulated him on the startling good looks of his children, but never forgot that he had to get them all married and in some cases he forced his will on a reluctant daughter. Strangely inconsistent when he had flouted all convention with his own marriage. We may wonder why Grace did not step in and defend a poor daughter about to be pushed into a loveless marriage.

Sabine worshipped his mother, and would jump to do her bidding. He was deeply saddened by her attitude when she failed to support his desire to go into the Church, despite her own devout faith. I suppose the unwritten rules concerning the elder and younger sons' roles were too strong for her. Both of the younger sons refused to take holy orders, and eventually both parents allowed Sabine to do so.

He was desperately impoverished at times, without food or lodgings, and his father refused to give him any kind of allowance. He had had it the hard way, and this may well have influenced his behaviour with his own children. He had his favourites, and made no excuse for this. Yet all his children admired him and fiercely defended his failings. They were thrown onto each other for protection, a tightly-knit and united team of brothers and sisters, who fought each other's battles. There was a huge discrepancy between their ages. Mary, the eldest, had her own child while her mother was still bearing children, yet she took great care of her younger brothers and sisters – as they all did.

When they were hurt, as in the case of my mother, it was covered up. He insisted that they have governesses to try and cram some knowledge into their unyielding brains. He seemed not to notice that none of the girls had any academic ability, yet they had real gifts in a variety of ways. They were all good-looking, and were known as "the lovely Baring-Gould girls".

Sabine had a sardonic humour and was a wicked tease. Sometimes his teases were basic and cruel and on many occasions he played jokes on an unsuspecting victim with a harsh sense of humour. Many of Sabine's jokes have been recorded. On one occasion his grandson Teddy turned the tables on him and when he found out, Sabine took it in good heart.

Running through the harsh side of his character was a deeply loving and spiritual side. His great interest in humanity, his compassion for their hard lot, his kindness to his servants and consideration for their welfare were all real. He was a good landlord. He shouldered colossal levels of expenditure. How he managed on his miserable stipend, small rents from his farms and the pittance from the sale of his books is amazing. He achieved a great deal on the sums available. Lew Trenchard house, then at the beginning of his ownership was a far cry from the house he left behind some forty years later, as well as the much improved state of the church.

Sabine Baring-Gould's writings were prolific. He always seemed to be writing something, even if it were not to become a book. His books were written to make money, but they earned relatively little, however popular they became. There was much abuse and cheating and plagiarism, with little redress. A book might bring something like £60, and many of them did not make that much. He wrote of Charles Dickens' work, and how he was cheated out of his rights by printers and administrators of his literary works. I gather this refers to the *Christmas Story* which sold in thousands, but the author received nothing. Sabine received similar treatment and was justifiably angry.

I have the inner feeling that Sabine had a deep grasp of the ancient Spiritual teachings. His devout beliefs, the respect, the ritualistic form of worship performed with deepest reverence; his interest in the Saints as messengers of the God he worshipped so profoundly – all this made him intolerant of the form of church worship he encountered with his peers. He was fiercely angry when he came across any form of spiritual hypocrisy. He writes scathingly of some of his contemporaries and was thus unpopular with the authorities of his day. He had nothing but contempt for the Church elders and did not fear to voice his opinions.

He had met with so little caring interest or support from his mother as a child and such insensitive authoritarianism from his father that he naturally became a "loner". He developed a skin to protect himself. He survived until his wife died, and then he collapsed. He seemed to lose his bearings and his purpose in life. The years after the Great War were dark ones for him. All the old rules were gone, and it was a new and ugly world. Everything – ambitions, standards, codes – seemed to have collapsed.

Bickford Dickinson says in his book that it would have been better for Sabine if he had gone before the War, when he was at the height of his fame and glory.

We will judge him for what he achieved. It was an amazing contribution to the life of his times. I only wish I had had the chance of meeting him, although I would not have had the years to understand the great man for what he had done. But I and my brother would have been grandchildren, and we might have seen the beautiful loving vision of the real man inside the ugly Victorian veneer he wore. He should be judged by his achievements for the benefit of posterity. He preserved so much which would undoubtedly have been lost. He did not waste a moment of his precious life; he filled every living moment; a remarkable man. I believe he would have been the greater had he had the benefits which we all have today, with our more liberal thinking.

Te Deum Gloria!

****

Onward, Christian soldiers!
   Marching as to war,
With the cross of Jesus
   Going on before.
Christ the royal Master
   Leads against the foe;
Forward into battle,
   See, his banners go;

Onward Christian soldiers,
Marching as to war.
With the cross of Jesus
Going on before.

At the sign of triumph
   Satan's legions flee;
On then, Christian soldiers,
   On to victory!
Hell's foundations quiver
   At the shout of praise;
Brothers, lift your voices,
   Loud your anthems raise;

Like a mighty army
   Moves the church of God;
Brothers, we are treading
   Where the saints have trod;

We are not divided,
   All one body we,
One in hope and doctrine,
   One in charity:

Crowns and thrones may perish,
   Kingdoms rise and wane,
But the Church of Jesus
   Constant will remain;
Gates of hell can never
   'Gainst that Church prevail;
We have Christ's own promise,
   And that cannot fail

Onward Christian soldiers,
Marching as to war,
With the cross of Jesus
Going on before.

THE MANA OF THE MANOR OF LEWE

The following is a deliberate "play" with words.

Mana. Or
Manna. Or
Manor...

The spelling is immaterial. The Dictionary refers to "mana" as "Food from Heaven". Also it expresses it in this way: "What is it?" Next they say it is "The Super Power" or "The Omnipotent GodForce"....

or The substance of life. The Bible records the story that this "Bread from Heaven" was fed to the fleeing Israelites. The interpretation of this story in this hidden text means "Inspiration through prayer (meditation) was given to the fleeing Israelites, to allow them to escape their oppressors."

In the Kahunna book of religions, "mana (manna)" is expressed as the substance of life. This substance is the Divine gift from the Creator. To renew this substance, it is mandatory to pray daily. (ie to meditate daily), to renew "the prayer endings" (perhaps by chanting). In modern language, this means to meditate or to go into a deep state of contemplation, thus able to contact the Creator.

To put this into our language, it means in this way it is to become inspired with this thought. To CREATE THROUGH THIS DIVINE INSPIRATION...(All manifested ideas are inspired by the Creator of ALL ideas). This essence of the Creator is there to provide the "Mana" or the substance or needs to live. Substance is the word we use to describe the way we create our livelihood. In essence we create the ideas. We have then to work out the way to develop these inspired thoughts, to make our lives expand, to deliver the very needs of our existence. This IS the food of life, all material developments are the result of thought, someone has thought the idea out, after, we presume, a great deal of inner contemplation, to produce the end result. ie the mana!

To return to the adaptation of the essence of a word. The Manorial House – the centre, which supplied the substance of a community as part of the Manorial Grant.

Mammon...In a commercial world, Mana is the financial reward (food) of life. It is the PAYMENT in living "substance" to those who have created the product of their inspiration. It is sometimes referred to as Mammon, meaning "riches". I.e. The God of riches.

To move to another word play: The word LEW.

Or is it LEWE? Or "Leuye" or "Ley", or is it just LE or "lane" or "lee" or the French word "le" meaning "the"? Or just a route or pathway or road?

Supposing we use the two letters LE as the root letters, then add on some directional signs such as the letter Y. This in sign language (coding) could denote a fork in the route or lane, i.e. a capital Y, if it is important. A small letter if it is not so, maybe indicating a small fork or twist.

We move to another directional sign: "I". Could this mean in this hidden code, "inner"?

Now try the letter U. Is that "under" or "up"? We will try the letter A, as "above" or maybe "again". The sign of an O – is this meaning to travel in a circle, or does it mean a circular route? The sign of a zigzag...a changing line?

These are some of the words with which we can "play" as having a far deeper meaning than the apparent surface value.

The changing spelling may have been caused by illiteracy of past decades, or was it possible that this was a deliberate policy to use as directional signs for those who knew what they were looking for. During the war years we took down our signposts deliberately to confuse the enemy. In this case, could these changes in spelling be part of a plan to preserve something very important, known only to the inner groups of highly educated wise individuals, such as the known scholars and priests of these times? This information, if this is the case, MUST have been so devastatingly important a source of information that they were united in their attempts to keep the secrets hidden, to prevent the uninitiated from corrupting this "something".

It must have been of great importance, that it needed such deep and involved a form of concealment. Those who wanted power for themselves who had not purified their motives, could have used this "something" for mischievous ends. Was it being kept away from the "dark forces", whoever they might be?

I have personally only recently stumbled on some of these deeper inner meanings behind words and coded pictures. I make these "hints" deliberately, and hope someone will find out more than I have done. What it is that is being coded...i.e. to quote the dictionary, "WHAT IS IT?"

The ancient Mystery Schools, used by the Essenes, Saumerians, Kahunnas, Egyptians and in the ancient Cabbala (Quabella), these word and picture signs possess a deep significance. Many similarities come through this ageless pattern of time. The coding is very similar in all forms of these ancient schools. They had a great religious reverence for the powers of The Earth and of the Great Creator. They knew that the balance of order was vital for the preservation of the fragile coexistence of all life forms. Persecution was the order of the day for those who dared blaspheme or believe anything but the current laws formed by rulers of the day. Religious persecution was of the most vicious form. This sent this ancient knowledge underground. The Mystery Schools trained their initiates to learn this inner language, to perpetuate these teachings to this day. Over the centuries there have been some selected Souls who have been aware of this need and have become hidden members of one or other of the Schools.

The coded signs or the subjects they chose were simple pictures from everyday life, so they would not attract attention, such as shepherdesses, lambs, birds of plumage, skeletons, gravestones, circles, crosses formed in certain ways, zigzag lines intersecting other lines, etc.

Many of these were very macabre, such as skeletons, skulls, gravestones. Some were plain dull pictures of fat unshapely shepherdesses. Although superficially boring, painted in such a way as to represent the subject's face, there was a double meaning based on the posture and/or positioning of several objects in the picture.

In this way the "Initiate" or scholar of these schools would know where to look. He or she would be able to decode it. The ancient man, perhaps even stone age man, knew far more than we do today. He built stone markers to indicate "something" . Was it a route map or did it say something else? Why are they so geometrically accurate, if they were a haphazard method of signposting? There was something exciting lying waiting down there for us all...what was it?

A panel from Lew House

My prompting was awakened by a remark a friend made to me while I was showing her around Lew Trenchard church, two or three years ago.

"Your Grandfather Sabine was some man! Was he a member of the mystery schools? Look!" she said, pointing to at least four simple pictograms in the windows and on the floor of the church.

"There is your sign that he knew that this place, this church and his home, is upon a very powerful energy line. perhaps it was he who coded these for us today, to begin our research today. He was living in a time of great restrictions upon men of the central institution of the Church. He could have lost his ministry and his church, had they known his true beliefs."

After that conversation I remembered that there were some strange pictures in Lew House. Ghoulish I thought them, as others obviously had done, as they were hidden away in the attic. One of a very dull (I thought) and boring stylised shepherdess, the oil fading on a rural scene, giving an outline of some scenery. Where is that picture now? Broken up as being of no value, as it looked on the outside. Another picture was of a skeleton killing a man in armour. Another was of a man praying in semi-darkness in a cave with the usual streaming light at the opening at the far end. Meaning, the praying man could see the end of his journey on earth. The other meanings can be deciphered, if you want to understand a bit more.

I myself have a very cursory knowledge of these hidden unproven things. I knew that I felt happy with the idea of "energy lines", known to me as Ley Lines, for want of a better word. These lines, it appears from researchers whjo use dowsing rods, etc. usually run through churches. In this way, prayer endings, chantings, hymns, psalms, etc., needed to be contained in a building to hold the resonance (echo?). In addition to a building, these lines seem to require a water spring or catchment. It seems that the activity of this bubbling water had a movement, a ceaseless movement, day and night, which apparently activates the energy in some strange way. Many ancient churches had water springs, usually termed a "holy well", either named by a Saint or after a Saint. They were reputed to generate healing powers. Could this be because the energy line flowed through it or around it and brought a new lease of life?

Lew had a Sacred Well which was reputed to have healing powers. It was located in the woods close by the church (or was it "A" – above the church?). Unfortunately it was moved into the lower gardens of Lew House. Presumably it became overgrown and neglected in its original site.

The church is on a "forked way". "The Y" curves from Lew Down and moves off to Marystowe via Chillaton. It is now known that these "lines" are like all electrical energy, requiring a male/female flow, or a negative/positive polarity. The turning off to Marystowe is West, so we have some new letters to add to LE... A (above), the fork Y, adding perhaps the W to travel West for

The Sacred Well

the female church (?) or do we travel along that route "N" or North? Was this new letter leading us to another church, the other side of Lew Down (N, or North). Lew Down could be in this instance Lew Down+N. perhaps Bratton Clovelly – a "Mary Church". Note the Mary Churches were named in Christian times, but if these had been built by the Celts, they would have had a female name other than Mary.

I will bring these suppositions to a close. You can see that I am very new at this form of research. I would rather leave it to those who have spent a great deal more time in this work to follow on and develop this theme. I am convinced that Sabine knew all about the ANCIENT WAY, and that he had been initiated in one or other of the Mystery Schools.

Sabine made three vows upon inheriting the house.

1. To repair, restore and preserve the Church.

2. To restore the house and property.

3. To serve his God and to look after his parishioners, and to give Glory to his Creator.

I feel it explains his almost fanatic desire to research, record and develop and to restore and promote interest. I feel he knew the mystery of the area. Is it magnetically charged with Earth's natural energies? Is that the magnetic appeal which draws so many to visit his work, life and vision for his home? He certainly magnetised the place with his own particular teachings and essence.

This little booklet records some of the lives of those who have lived in this tiny spot on the face of the Earth. I leave it to my readers to work out how much each individual gave back to the "power" of the Earth with their lives. Was it a Plus or a Minus?

I may have a fanciful belief. I have a theory...no I believe profoundly that there is an intricate pattern in our lives and I believe in the Law of Cause and Effect. This is the Biblical story of the saying "As you sow, so shall you reap". I also believe that we are united in some magnificent way into a huge group SOUL family, so large we know not its limits. With this idea goes that we do not have to be linked by something far stronger, perhaps by a soundwave, or waveband of energy.

It is an intensely complicated theme, but it seems awesome in its mathematical precision. I have noted that apparent strangers have walked into the house, and have had a deep memory, stirred by an awareness, a will o' the wisp thread of something which brings a sense of deep emotion, some good and some bad. They make unsolicited and/or startling statements, which only a member of the family could verify, as being a strange coincidence. Are these people really strangers to the house, or did they know it in some long forgotten day? I believe that they have been called back to "earth" their energies, to restore some part of either themselves or the house, land or church; a part of the past which may have been destroyed; a part of the Soul journey. It is a cleansing in some baptismal way. These vital energies which we know so desperately little about, may be restoring the most vital part of ourselves. I pray that soon we will glimmer the real truth and act fast to change our ways and help heal this Planet, walking this earth with care.

FAMILY TREE

EDWARD III = PHILIPPA OF HAINAULT
KING OF ENGLAND

LIONEL OF ANTWERP = LADY ELIZABETH DE BURGH
DUKE OF CLARENCE

EDMUND DE MORTIMER = PHILIPPA OF CLARENCE
3RD EARL OF MARCH

ROGER 4TH EARL OF MARCH = LADY ELEANOR HOLLAND

RICHARD EARL OF CAMBRIDGE = LADY ANNE MORTIMER

HENRY 2ND COUNT OF EU, 1ST = LADY ISABEL PLANTAGANET
EARL OF ESSEX

WILLIAM VISCOUNT BOURCHIER = LADY ANNE WYDEVILLE

JOHN 8TH LORD FERRERS OF CHARTLEY = CECILY BOURCHIER

WALTER 1ST VISCOUNT HEREFORD = LADY MARY GREY

SIR RICHARD DEVEREUX = LADY DOROTHEA HASTINGS

WALTER 1ST EARL OF ESSEX = LETTICE KNOLLYS

ROBERT 3RD LORD RICH = LADY PENELOPE DEVEREUX

HENRY 1ST EARL OF HOLLAND = ISABEL COPE

WILLIAM 6TH LORD PAGET = LADY FRANCES RICH

ROWLAND HUNT = FRANCES PAGET

THOMAS HUNT = JANE WARD

THOMAS HUNT = SARAH WITTS

JOSEPH SABINE = SARAH HUNT

WILLIAM BARING-GOULD = DIANA AMELIA SABINE

EDWARD BARING-GOULD = SOPHIA CHARLOTTE BOND

REV. SABINE BARING-GOUND = GRACE TAYLOR

GRACE BARING-GOULD (née Taylor)

Grace met the handsome thirty-year-old Sabine when she was only sixteen years old. He, evidently, was completely overwhelmed with her tiny form and startlingly beautiful barley-sugar-coloured hair. He had never met anyone like her before; she was modest, yet she had a sparkling humour in a puckish way that would burst out of her unexpectedly. Her hilarity never failed to delight her listeners. She had little or no education, and when she met Sabine she had a broad Yorkshire accent, with a lovely lilt to it.

She was evidently impressed by Sabine's scholarly ways and his amazing good looks. He was tall and slim, with blond hair and clear blue eyes. She was not intimidated by his obvious academic abilities, nor by his social background, which was worlds away from hers. Her own life as the child of a poor mill worker, and herself a mill hand, had taken a very different form from his.

Their rapid and deep attachment to each other created a complete rift with families on both sides. When they decided to marry, not one member of either side was represented – there was a complete refusal to acknowledge the situation. Later, Sabine appears to have been penalised for his inappropriate marriage, and sent to difficult parishes. They went to Dalton for a short time, then East Mersea in Essex, a flat and windy place. In their different ways, each loved the moors – she those of Yorkshire, and he Dartmoor – and this was a sad time for them.

Grace

It must have been a most frightening experience for the young bride, still only seventeen, when she became pregnant almost immediately, miles from her own people. She had chosen to live with a difficult and eccentric older man, and was constantly pregnant with a baby every year. She was often delivered of her babies alone, Sabine being away on one of his trips.

There is a story told that she contacted the cleric who had married them at Horbury Brig, to ask him to *unmarry* them! She found Sabine's temper and incompetence around the house too much to put up with.

One's heart aches for her. Prior to her marriage, Sabine had seen fit to have her sent to some relatives who were exceedingly respectable (and no doubt excessively boring), to have poor lovely Grace taught how to be a lady. She had to learn how to eat and how to lose her broad Yorkshire dialect. She was an apt pupil, as I have heard accounts of her as a most gentle refined gracious lady, who gave no indication of her humble origins. She never lost her aching love for her beloved Yorkshire moors, and could not see the beauty of Dartmoor, thinking it wet and forbidding. She told my mother of her yearnings, when she lay on her sick bed, often in a darkened room.

On their Continental honeymoon, Sabine insisted they spend their leisure hours looking at churches and other Gothic buildings, until Grace rebelled and refused to look at any more. Poor insensitive Victorian male that he was! But he did buy her a bonnet as a treat. Perhaps he thought this bit of frivolity would lift her sad spirits and loneliness.

Sabine adored her, but he had a Victorian attitude in his expectations of her – shouldering all responsibility for running his house. She was always short of money, although frugal and a good manager. Her early years of poverty had helped her to learn to live with this "will o' the wisp" man she had married. His extravagant tastes did make her angry, as she thought them wasteful.

Despite these shortcomings in their relationship, he evidently considered her words of wisdom on many occasions. She could often persuade him out of a rash act, and he respected her remarks. But he was often away from home for days on end, with no possibility of communicating with her, or returning quickly if needed. He often changed his plans, and she must have been concerned at times for his safety. At the same time her own responsibilities were growing, with the increasing size of her family.

Sabine spent his money elsewhere and on other things. Grace was left to run the house, feed and clothe the children, and pay the servants. She never complained openly, and was greatly respected by people from every station in life. On one occasion, she asked Sabine to buy meat for the family, telling him the weight. He forgot what she had said and came back with an entire side of a bullock. Grace was upset by this wastefulness, and did her best to use it all. They ended up by eating beef so many times that even Sabine complained.

It is my belief that Grace, with her beautiful simplicity and purity of spirit, as a child of Victorian England, would have found the subject of sex quite taboo. Any discussion of this matter, with Sabine or any confidante, would have been considered immodest and indecent. We can only guess at her feelings, when she had to submit to Sabine's ardour, knowing so little of procreation. She made an enlightening comment to my mother when close to death. Cicely had returned from her own two-day honeymoon, and expressed herself upset with Grace for not warning her about the marriage night. Grace, some fifty years after her own honeymoon, simply said, in great embarrassment, "I did not want to lose the respect of you or any of my daughters."

Sabine, with his limited awareness of the sensitivities of marriage and the shock his wife must be feeling, would doubtless have been nonplussed by the situation. Sex was his way of showing Grace his enduring love and faithfulness, perhaps a way of making up for his frequent trips away from home. When she was ill at the end of her life, bedridden and in great pain, his visits to her were perfunctory, with just a peck on the cheek. Her health and welfare were not discussed; it was not his department – others would care for her better than he. I am sure he would have been shocked if he had realised the hurt he was giving to her. He really did adore her and she never complained or asked him for help.

My mother looked after her over her last years. Cicely saw a great deal of the inner situation between her parents. She, like her brothers and sisters, had a huge respect for Sabine, but she could see his flaws, and she agonised for the welfare of her beloved and frail mother. When asked why she had so many children, Grace said simply that they were the natural *fruiting* of her marriage. It was only in the latter years that she put together the act of sex and the birth of babies. A nursery nurse took over her babies as they were weaned. She said rather poignantly that she wished she could be like her daughters who had only two or three babies, so that she might have managed to nurse them herself. She actually asked her daughters how they managed to keep the numbers down.

Grace told my mother that she found Lew House dark and depressing. She hated Devonshire mists and eternal rain. The continuous building programme wore her down. Her son Edward in 1912 installed central heating for her in Lew House, because she was always so cold. Alas, the system was badly installed and never functioned properly. Edward offered to get the man back and put it right, but she declined, preferring to avoid more workmen in the house. This is an insight into her real feelings, poor lovely lady.

This little story is revealing:Edward and Marion were in London and had Grace to stay with them. They offered to take her to the theatre, wanting her to have some life away from Lew. Yes, she would like that very much, but please, no classics. She would love to go to a burlesque show!

What did she put up with, silently? Her children grew up without a mother's warmth, she was so occupied elsewhere. She had her last baby when she was forty-five, at the time very ill. Her poor fingers were gnarled and twisted and her body was soon to follow suit. Her only personal woman friend was Mrs Sperling of Coombe Trenchard. It was a terrible time of genteel hypocritical snobbishness. She remained detached as much as possible, yet no one ever forgot her humble beginnings. Even though she could not be faulted in her work as the Lady of the Manor, giving gentle concern to everyone.

It is thought that G.B. Shaw's *Pygmalion* was inspired by his experience at Lew Trenchard, and meeting Grace. She was more a lady than many of the socialised gentry of the times. Many literary giants of the day were guests at Lew Trenchard and were charmed by their lovely unassuming hostess. In particular they were enchanted with her melodious voice, which had no trace of her Yorkshire background. Many times have I been told of the softness and warmth of her voice.

Women's lot in Victorian times was hard. Romance could not have lasted long. Grace died in 1916, before her husband, released from very painful rheumatoid arthritis. Sabine went to pieces after her death. His work deteriorated. His epitaph to his wife was very beautiful: "To half of my Life". *DIMIDIUM ANIMAE MEAE*

The Family Tree

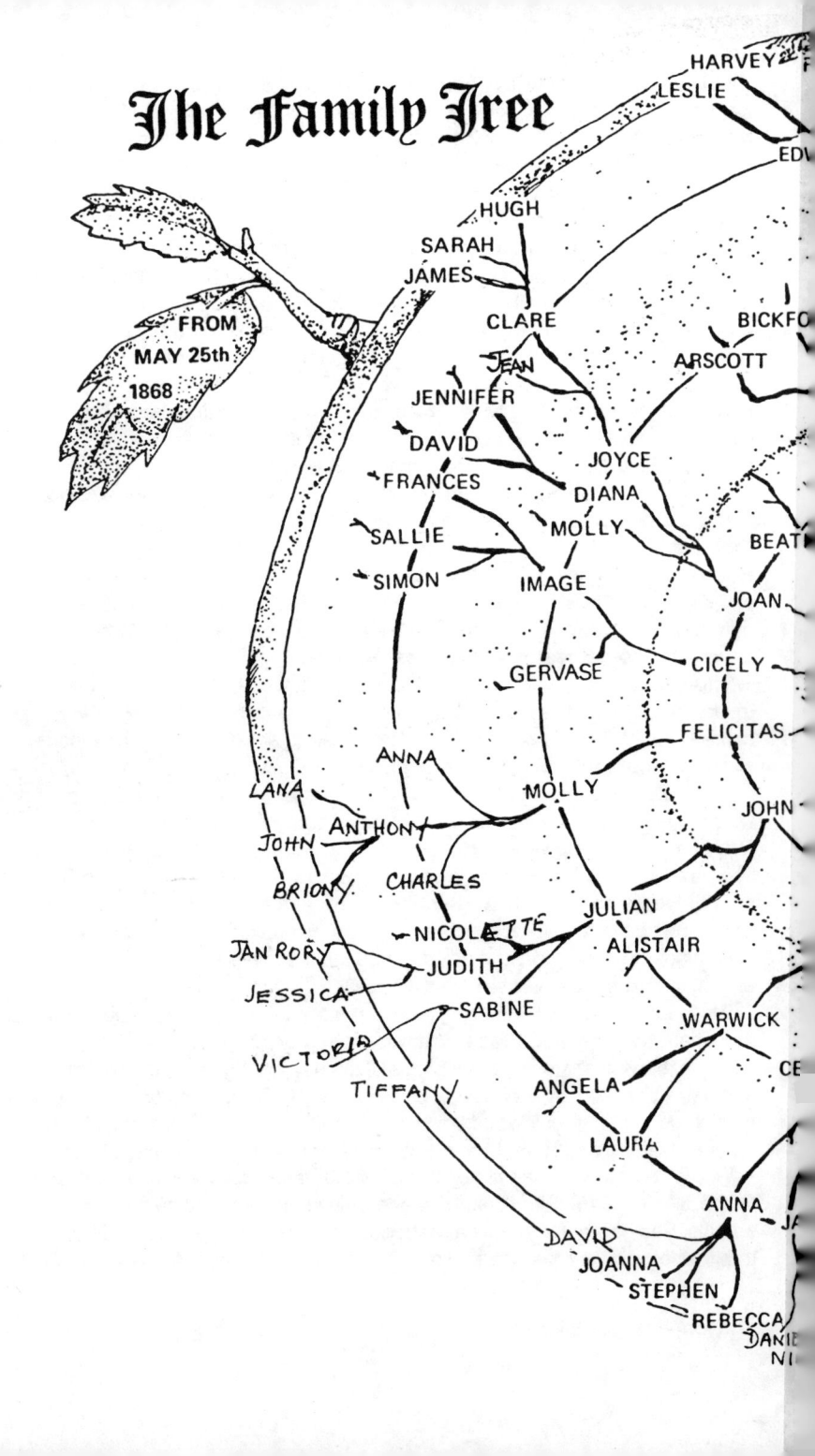

FROM MAY 25th 1868

HARVEY
LESLIE
EDW
HUGH
SARAH
JAMES
CLARE
BICKF
JEAN
ARSCOTT
JENNIFER
DAVID
JOYCE
FRANCES
DIANA
SALLIE
MOLLY
BEAT
SIMON
IMAGE
JOAN
CICELY
GERVASE
FELICITAS
ANNA
MOLLY
JOHN
LANA
ANTHONY
JOHN
CHARLES
BRIONY
NICOLETTE
JULIAN
JAN RORY
ALISTAIR
JUDITH
JESSICA
SABINE
VICTORIA
WARWICK
TIFFANY
CE
ANGELA
LAURA
ANNA
DAVID
JA
JOANNA
STEPHEN
REBECCA
DANIE
NI

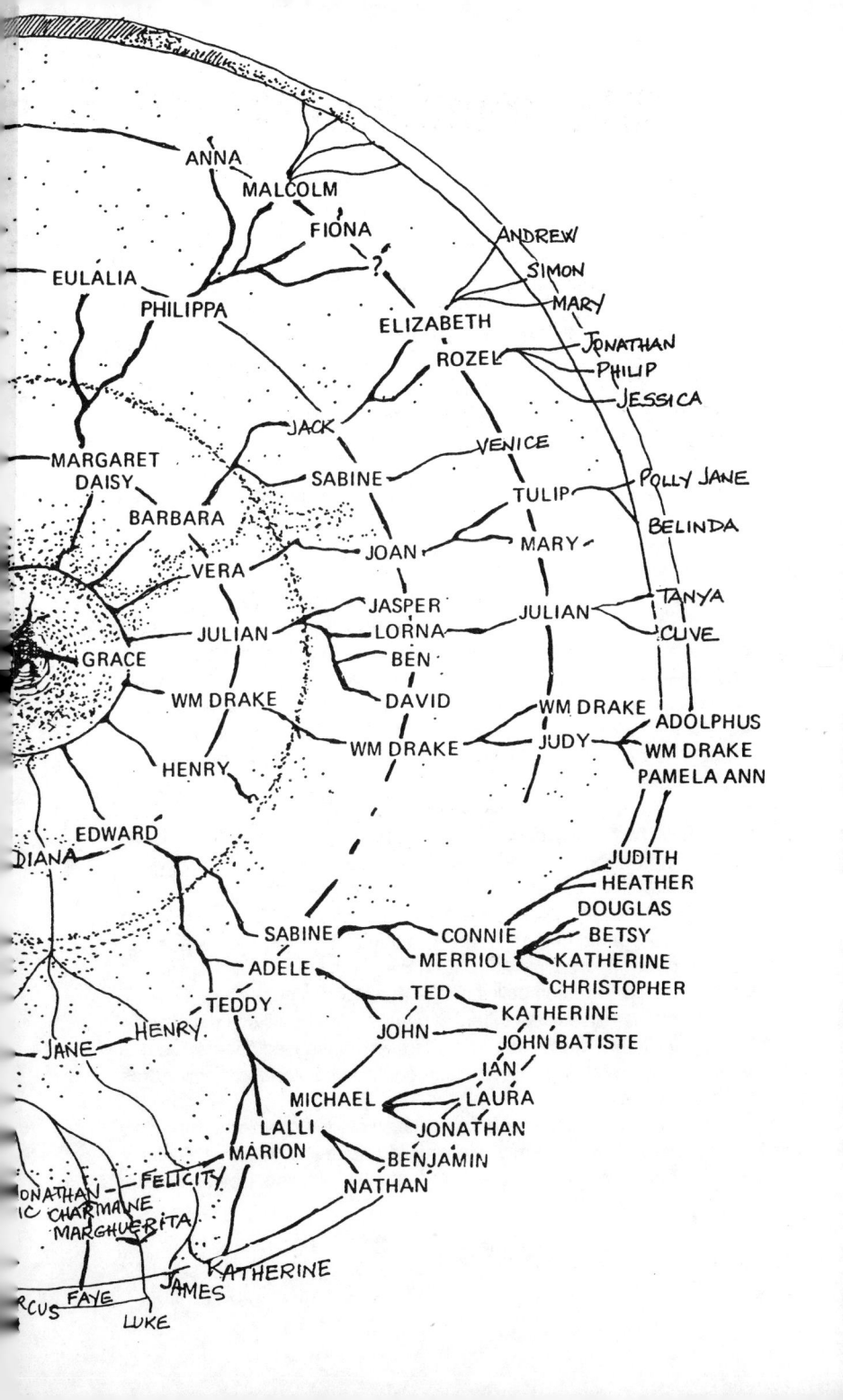

ANNA
MALCOLM
FIONA
?
ANDREW
SIMON
MARY
EULALIA
PHILIPPA
ELIZABETH
ROZEL
JONATHAN
PHILIP
JESSICA
JACK
VENICE
MARGARET
DAISY
SABINE
TULIP
POLLY JANE
BELINDA
BARBARA
JOAN
MARY
VERA
JASPER
JULIAN
TANYA
JULIAN
LORNA
CLIVE
GRACE
BEN
WM DRAKE
DAVID
WM DRAKE
ADOLPHUS
WM DRAKE
JUDY
WM DRAKE
HENRY
PAMELA ANN

EDWARD
JUDITH
HEATHER
DIANA
DOUGLAS
SABINE
CONNIE
BETSY
ADÈLE
MERRIOL
KATHERINE
TEDDY
TED
CHRISTOPHER
KATHERINE
JANE
HENRY
JOHN
JOHN BATISTE
IAN
MICHAEL
LAURA
LALLI
JONATHAN
MARION
BENJAMIN
JONATHAN
FELICITY
NATHAN
IC
CHARMAINE
MARGUERITA
KATHERINE
RCUS
FAYE
JAMES
LUKE

LEW TRENCHARD HOUSE
Its origins and construction

The mouldings were worked with putty and lime finely sieved and mixed with horsehair. The lines of ornamentation were made with ribbons of copper or lead. The design was fashioned through this technique. The huge plaster drops were bolted to the rafters, which had to be reinforced due to the excessive weight.

The house was originally built from local stone, quarried from the hill behind the house, and the slates for the roof were also local, cut by local workers.

The woodland was systematically cultivated to supply all the needs of the Estate. In the case of Lew House, in the early days the house was set in the heart of dense forest. Later, deliberate plantings of woodland was a policy of survival, and the relics of these woodlands still remain, although severed from the estate and leased out.

There has been some erroneous thinking surrounding the house since Sabine's day. It was his habit to collect regardless of the size of the object, and to place his trophy in whichever niche was empty. The result was thought by many to be haphazard and inappropriate. There is no doubt that he copied ideas from other great houses, but his motives were sound. He was determined to create a house of real interest and beauty, regardless of criticism. He was also concerned to rescue beautiful objects which might otherwise have been destroyed.

There were certainly some mistakes made along the way. Sabine was very poor at maths and had no architectural training. One example of miscalculation is the huge ill-fitting overmantel in the ballroom; another is the missing staircase in the new Rectory. The story of the latter is quite amusing – when he built the replacement Rectory, having sold Coombe Trenchard to the Sperlings, it had to be done in some haste. The curate was arriving soon, and needed a roof over his head. The building was almost complete when it was discovered that there was no main staircase. Sabine had forgotten to put it into the plans. There was a back staircase in place, but belatedly a more pretentious stair was crammed in off the hall, which has never looked to be in keeping with the house.

As it grew and gained in embellishments, Lew House created quite a stir. The snobbish element in society, after the War, labelled it a "Victorian hotch-potch". Right up to his death, this element often expressed themselves as appalled at the over-elaborations and disregard for the standard procedures and tastes of the day.

The actual original structure and foundations of Lew are clothed in misty and fragmentary scraps of history. Records do not tell us whether it was in the present location or in Lew Trenchard hamlet with the Dower House, which appears in *The Doomsday Book* (see page 4). There is a story that an Edward the Confesser coin was dug out of one of the walls during reconstruction, but it may have been a collector's piece.

Over the main fireplace, carved into the woodwork, are the intertwined initials of Henry and his wife Ann. They evidently went there for their honeymoon, having bought the house from Sir Thomas Monk. It is possible that the mantel first came from the Dower House. We know that Ann moved there when she was widowed.

Old "Madam" Gould stayed on in the house, not altering it in any way. Her husband had demolished a great section of the original house, wanting it smaller. It became a long, dull, low-storeyed place. We have a sketch of it at that period. But Madam did add some farmland and ably managed the estate farms. There are tales of her ghost still riding on her rounds of inspection. Sabine Baring-Gould's *Book of Folklore* tells one of these stories.

Neither William nor Edward cared about the house, and when Sabine came upon the scene it was in a deeply neglected state. It appears that he always had the idea of forming the house into an Elizabethan "E" shape, with three wings forming the cross pieces. We don't know what the significance of this may have been, if any. His researches indicated that there had been a house on the site for a considerable period of time. But who had built it originally, and was it in this shape?

Forty years of building later, the house had a strongly Elizabethan look with two wings around a courtyard.

In his *Book of Reminiscences* Sabine tells of a Christmas he spent with his brother Willy just after he inherited the house. They were plagued by rats, the house having been empty and neglected for years.

Sabine loved all old things and ancient crafts. He believed and proved that, given an opportunity, anyone could produce an object of great beauty. His point was demonstrated, and he began to fill his home and church with thr results of much local craft work, as well as some foreign artefacts. The great overmantle came from Austria, for example. Many benches, screens, windows were salvaged from far and wide, jolting back to Lew on wagons packed with straw.

Sabine, Old Madam and Ann Gould were the only owners who genuinely cared for the estate and worked for its maintenance and improvement. As we have seen, most of the others disliked and neglected the property. This became true again after 1932, when much was sold off or left to fall into disrepair.

Sabine's wife, Grace, lived with the mess and inconvenience of building work for almost the whole of her time at Lew. It must have been exhausting for her, and she told her daughter-in-law that she longed for peace and quiet.

During the Civil War, the family was divided between Parliamentarians and Royalists. It is thought that secret tunnels were made beneath the house at that time. The only one now visible is next to the main hall and the ballroom, above the door. It is believed that this was formerly the kitchen. There is an enormous fireplace behind all the carving, which links with the deep recessions by the corner of the fireplace in the room now used as the bar. We may imagine these tunnels linking up with the mineshafts running under the hill of Lew Down, although all evidence has disappeared.

Sabine more than fulfilled his dream, in the final creation of Lew House. It is a museum of the craftsman's arts, full of interest and beauty. It is now lovingly cared for, polished and tended. Sabine would be very pleased.

Lew House

THE CHILDREN OF GRACE AND SABINE

(See the family tree in the centre spread for the complete family)

1. **MARY**
   (Mrs Dickinson) Sons, Edward, Arscott and Bickford
2. **MARGARET** (Daisy)
   (Mrs Rowe) Daughters, Eulalia and Philippa
3. **EDWARD SABINE**
   Sons, Sabine Linton, Edward (Teddy); daughter, Adele
4. **BEATRICE**
   Died very young
5. **VERONICA**
   (Mrs King). Daughter, Joan. Grand-daughters, Mary and Tulip
6. **JULIAN**
   Sons, Jasper, Ben, David; daughter, Lorna
7. **WILLIAM**
   Son, William
8. **BARBARA**
   (Mrs Burnard). Sons, Sabine and Jack
9. **DIANA**
   (Mrs Batten.) Sons, Henry, Julian; daughter, Jane
10. **FELICITAS**
    (Mrs Ayre, then Mrs Berkeley-Wily). Daughter, Mona
11. **HENRY**
    Died unmarried in 1913 in Malaya
12. **JOAN**
    (Mrs Priestley) Daughters, Joyce, Diana, Mollie
13. **CICELY**
    (Mrs Newport Tinley) Son, Gervase; daughter, Cicely (Image)
14. **JOHN HILARY**
    Sons, Julian and Alistair
15. **GRACE**
    (Mrs Calmady-Hamlyn) Son, Warwick; daughter, Cecily

Mary Dickinson

Born in Dalton in 1869, she married Harvey Dickinson and lived at Dunsland with her family on a massive rundown impoverished estate. The house was interesting, dating back prior to the Doomsday records. It was ultimately purchased by (or given to) the National Trust, who brought it back to a fine state of repair. Alas, it caught fire only days after a tenant moved in and was totally gutted. A memorial stone now marks the spot. Mary and Harvey had three sons: Bickford, Arscott and Edward.

Bickford, the middle son, stayed at home while his mother was alive to help her manage the estate, as his father was not gifted in that way. Bick was very clever with his hands and modelled little boats in bottles, accurate in every detail. He had huge hands, but somehow achieved the most delicate work. Sadly, he lost his entire collection to the fire.

Talking of fire (and smoke), I remember as a small girl visiting Aunt Mary. She was most popular with us kids (she had a penchant for bull's eyes, and so did we!), and we used to sit in the library with a huge fire roaring up the chimney. The problem was that most of the smoke would return *down* the chimney, rather more than it went up. The room was forever clouded and the tears would run constantly from our eyes. Aunt Mary always managed to smile serenely through all this obvious discomfort. We noticed that her eyes were always dry.

Mary

In those days they lived a primitive life in this wonderful house. The roof was leaking so badly that they had to use an umbrella to go upstairs to bed! (This is true – I did it myself.)

Bickford wrote an interesting book on our grandparent called *Sabine Baring-Gould, Squarson, Writer, Folklorist* and published by David and Charles. He later wrote a book on his old home, which was never published, more's the pity. He went as master to Shebbear College, and married the music mistress, Madge. He eventually took to the cloth and became Rector of Lewtrenchard for a while. He and Madge had no children.

Arscott and his wife Eva were likewise childless. He was a wonderful caricaturist artist, and eventually became Librarian at St Helier, in Jersey.

Edward Dabernon went to Rhodesia and served in the police for a while. Then he went into tobacco, and finally printing. He and his wife Frances Ann have now retired to South Africa. They have two sons, Edward Arnold Baring and Sabine Harvey (Bill).

Margaret Rowe

Born in Dalton, in 1870, she was always known as Daisy. She had two daughters, Eulalia and Philippa. Eulalia married Guy Newman who had the incumbency of Lew Trenchard. They did not enjoy their stay in the Parish; the house was cold and uncomfortable.

Philippa is an interesting pioneer lady. She went to school in Innsbruck, and from there to Venice where she worked as a translator and language teacher. She soon became enamored with flying, and met and married an airman. She qualified as a pilot and ground engineer at the time Amy Mollison was making flying headlines. She used to scrub down her husband's planes and overhaul the engines, to make herself useful and keep herself in the forefront of aviation. She was well known by people in all the right place.

At one event, one of their parachutists and wing walkers was killed, and Philippa took his place until a replacement was found.

Margaret

Edward

Born in East Mersea in 1870. Married to Marion, he had three children, Sabine Linton, Teddy (Edward) and Grace Adele.

Sabine Linton inherited Lew House for a short period. Merriol and Connie are his two daughters by his first wife, Connie. Connie Junior has two daughters, Judith and Heather.

Grace Adele has a special section to herself further on in the booklet. See page 43

Teddy (Edward Darragh) lives in California with Barbara, his second wife. He has built up a business and is a keen fruit grower. He and Sabine, like his father before them, went away to the States as soon as they left their public schools, to earn very successful livings there. Teddy has had great attachments to his family in his family home and has been of great assistance to all of us over in the "ole Country" with his timely advice and help. He had three children from his first marriage to Sheena: Michael, Marion and Lally.

His only beloved son, Michael, was drowned at sea in Alaska. Teddy placed a memorial seat to him near the Church. Lally lives in Columbia and has two sons. Marion tragically died a few years ago.

There is a further section on Teddy. See page 44

These three were the last of the family to live with their parents at Lew House. They moved from the Rectory into the house after Grace died and Sabine was left helplessly alone.

Beatrice

Born in East Mersea in 1874, she died in 1876. She is said to haunt Lew House.

Veronica

Known as Vera, she was born in East Mersea in 1875, and married Dr Arthur King. He was a tall man, an old-time doctor who was also Master of the Tetcot Hunt. He was outspoken and a real tease. I thought him the finest of uncles, despite the endless ragging I received. Vera was a talented musician, yet she seldom played

Veronica

after she married. Arthur was tone deaf and loathed any form of music. They had one beloved daughter, Joan, who married Bob Radcliffe and had two daughters, Mary and Tulip. Both Joan and Mary died of cancer. Tulip now runs a smart guest house in Yorkshire, as well as being a landscape gardener. She has two daughters, Polly Jane and Belinda.

Julian

Born in East Mersea in 1877, he married Joan Ransden and they had four children. he worked for the Rajah of Sarawak (who came originally from Yelverton) for a while. Two of their sons, Benjamin and Jasper, went into the Tank Corps during the Second World War, and both were killed within a short time.

Lorna, their daughter, became a well-known miniature artist. She has one son, Julian. David, the third brother, died when young.

Julian

William Drake

William Drake

Born in East Mersea in 1878, he lived in America and became British Vice Consul in Minneapolis. He married Harriet Rollins Stuart and had one son, William Stuart, who became well known for his satirical writings. He worked for Time Inc., and married Lucile Marguerite Moody (Cecil). They had two children, a son, William Drake and a daughter Judith Ann. William Drake Jnr was killed in a car accident in 1966. Judith Ann married Adolphus Busch Orthwein Jnr and they have three children.

Barbara

Born at Lew Trenchard in 1880, she married Laurie Burnard. He was the son of Sabine's best friend, and is mentioned a great deal in his memoirs. They had two sons, Sabine and Jack. Sabine went to Australia, married and has a daughter Venice, who also lives in

Barbara

Diana

Australia.

Jack went eventually to Rhodesia, married Diana, and has two children, Elizabeth and Rosel. Elizabeth lives in Kent, with three children, Andrew, Simon and Mary. Rosel and her husband Patrick live in Devon, having spent some time in South Africa. They have three children, Jonathan, Philip and Jessica.

Diana Amelia

Born at Lew Trenchard in 1881, she married Hugh Maxwell–Batten and lived with him for a while in Borneo. They had three children, Jane, Henry and Julian. Jane (Cassels) had one daughter, Felicity (Craigen), who had two children, Katherine and James.

Henry lives in New Zealand and has two daughters. Julian and his wife Elizabeth live in Exeter and have five children, Jonathan, Charmaine (who had a daughter, Faye), Justin (son, Marcus), Dominic and Marghuerita (son, Luke).

Felicitas Ayre

Born at Lew Trenchard in 1883 and known as Titus to us all, she had one daughter, Mollie, from her first marriage. She was married a second time, to Frank Berkley Wylie.

Mollie became Mrs King and had three children, Anna, Charles and Anthony (Tony). Anna works as a therapist is alternative medicine and is unmarried. Anthony is an estate agent and auctioneer. He and Nicky have three children and live at Bradford near

Felicitas

Holsworthy.

Henry (Harry)
Born at Lew Trenchard in 1885, he had a very rough time working at the Bristol docks as a labourer and became very ill. He and a companion walked back to Lew Trenchard from Bristol to convalesce, but his father decided that he should find work as soon as possible. He went to Borneo and died of fever.

Joan
Born at Lew Trenchard in 1887, she married Bill Priestly and spent some years in India. They then moved to Scotland, where Bill owned an estate. They had three daughters, Joyce, Diana and Molly. It was due to Joan's interest in the family history that we have so much information today.

Joyce married George Rawstorn and had two daughters, Clare and Jean. Clare has three children and lives in London. Jean adopted two children, and unfortunately died in a riding accident. Diana married Geoff Snowden and has two children, Jennifer and David. Jennifer has Melanie and William. Molly did not marry and lived in Ireland for a time, but is now living in the Isle of Wight.

Joan

John

Cicely
Born at Lew Trenchard in 1889, she married Frank Newport Tinley and went out to India. Frank was in the Indian cavalry. She intensely disliked the life, despite being a crack shot and keen horsewoman. They had two children, Cicely (Image) and Gervase, who were sent back to England for their schooling at a very tender age. They were left in the care of relatives as guardians.

Image married Godfrey Charles Briggs and had three children: Simon, Sallie and Frankie. Gervase left school and joined the RAF at nineteen, and like his cousins, Ben and Jasper, was killed after being shot down twice. He qualified as a pilot flying Pathfinders, dropping troops and intelligence personnel behind enemy lines. The first time he was shot down, in the English Channel, he was given ten days' rest and then sent back to resume work. His nerves were shaken and no doubt he had a terrifying time returning to all that flak. He was shot down in flames and with all his crew, died over Holland. He got the DFC and bar posthumously.

There is a special tribute to Cicely on page 61

John
Born at Lew Trenchard in 1890, he married Nancy and had two sons, Alistair and

Julian. They lived in Rhodesia. John was a great craftsman, building furniture, boats and even gun casings. Alistair died young from nephritis.

Julian lives in Somerset West in South Africa with his wife Dawn. He has inherited his father's great gifts as a craftsman. Julian and Dawn have three children, Nicolette, Judith and Sabine. They all live in South Africa and Zimbabwe. Judith and Sabine each have two children.

Grace

Grace

Born at Lew Trenchard in 1891, was the last child. She married Charles Calmady Hamlyn from the adjoining estate of Leawood, Bridestowe. She suffered acutely from rheumatoid arthritis from a very early age, a deadly inheritance from her mother. She endured many painful operations but remained sweet-tempered and gentle to the end. She and Charles had two children: Cecily, who married Lambert and had three children (Anna, Jane and John) and Warwick, who has two daughters from his second marriage, to Joan (Laura and Angela).

Warwick was in the regular Army, stationed in India for a while. After he left the Army he returned to take over the management of Leawood estates. His daughter Laura has a son.

The other branch of the family.

Through his second marriage to Lavinia Snow, Edward Baring-Gould ("The Silver Poplar") had two children, Arthur and Leila. Arthur had three children, Irene, Cedric and Dora. Leila married Frank Carver and had two sons, Frank and Jack.

Irene Widdecombe is the matriarch of a large family of descendants. She lives in Stanmore, London, has a keen memory, and is over ninety years old. Two of her memories of Uncle Sabine and Aunt Grace and of the Church throw a very interesting light on the behaviour of the day. They are reproduced in full in the following section.

Dora (Waters) has an only son, Chris, who lives in Saunders Town, USA. Cedric lives in Sussex, is married with two children.

Leila's son Frank was killed in the Great War in France. Jack has two daughters, Flora (Liesa) and Penelope Leila, and a son Jeane Jacques who died very young from bone cancer. Flora married Alec Brown, and has two sons. She lives in the Isle of Wight, having been brought up by her grandmother Leila.

There is a small family booklet on this side of the family. It gives a delightful insight into the fine relationship between Lavinia and her much beloved son.

Grace Adele

Grace Adele Baring-Gould was born on June 11th 1905. She grew up at Lew Trenchard with her brothers Sabine and Teddy, living in the Rectory until she went away to school in her early teens. The children's closest friend was Roger Arundell, son of the Revd. Sabine Baring-Gould's curate, Gilbert Arundell. The curate taught the children before they went away to school, and was much loved by them.

Adele must have known her grandfather well, as he was also living in the house at the time. The story goes that he "glorified" the ballroom especially to make it suitable for her Coming Out Ball. The event is referred to in Bickford Dickinson's book (see Page ***). There are not many of us who can claim to have had a room especially recreated for our own dance. It must have been an amazing event.

After the War, new arrangements were made for the big house, with Sabine getting old and difficult. Marion must have found this hard to bear, and probably badly needed the company of her daughter.

Adele loved the countryside and was fond of gardening and animals, especially her dogs. She acted as driver for her mother and led a group of Girl Guides from the area. She had an excellent mind, and the Head of her boarding school urged her parents to enable her to go to Cambridge University as her brothers had done. But Edward vetoed this, presumably because of her gender.

Adele had a passion for horticulture, and it is due to her that there are many thousands of daffodils tumbling down the banks and lawns of Lew. There is a little stream running through the garden which still illustrates her handiwork. She planted all kinds of interesting species in the woods at the back of the house as well as in the garden. Marion and her sister Gertrude also did a great deal to add to the beauty of the house and gardens.

In the early 1930s when Marion had died, Adele followed her brothers to America. She studied cytology and microbiology and was certfied as a medical technician by the New York State Health Department. For several years she worked at the New York Hospital as a technician for Dr Papanicolaou, an unappreciated researcher who eventually developed a method for detecting cervical cancer in women. His work has since saved hundreds of thousands of lives.

In 1937, Adele married Jack Reboul and they have two sons, John and Edward (Ted). At their country house near St James, Long Island, Jack and Adele were accomplished gardeners, specialising in rhododendrons. Adele develoiped, showed and patented several new varieties, naming two of them after Jack and her grand-daughter Kathryn. She has always taken a strong interest in her community, in women's issues, animals and above all, the environment.

Teddy

I wish to conclude this section with a tribute to Edward, Teddy, Baring-Gould, my most beloved and dear cousin, who lives in California. Teddy, as he is known to all of us, and Teddy Bear to his devoted grandchildren, IS totally a part of this house. He lived here as a child and young man. His personality is deeply imprinted in the stones and mortar of the place and although he has been an exile from his English home and has lived in the States for the best part of his life. He IS Lew Trenchard and always will be. It is due to his keen interest and love for the family that Merriol and I and all the rest of us have been drawn together in a fine united family.

May I be forgiven a personal note, and record a small event which took place in 1930. Teddy kept the records – I, the faithless one, did not! That year, my brother Gervase and I came to live at Lew with Marion Baring-Gould, Teddy, Sabine and Adele's mother. Our parents were stationed in India and we were homeless waifs. I fell passionately in love with Lew, with Aunt Marion and with Teddy. I was ten years old and no doubt was a horrible precocious child, who decided that my devastatingly

Teddy

handsome cousin Teddy should be persuaded to enter into a contract of marriage with me. Why he should think that a ten-year-old girl with pigtails should be worth even the faintest recognition is amazing!

I wrote him a letter of proposal, and to his great and lasting credit he has kept the letter to this day [written in 1979] – fifty years later. At the time he courteously acknowledged my letter, accepting my proposal and enclosing a ring. Faithless, careless me! I lost the ring and the letter, but I have never lost my respect and love for my dearest and most beloved cousin.

MEMORIES OF IRENE WIDDECOMBE
UNCLE SABINE AND AUNT GRACE

I am one of the very few left who knew that fabulous pair, Sabine and Grace. They could not have been more different – a most unlikely match – yet, I think it was one of the most wonderful marriages in history. They were completely devoted to each other.

I could never describe them to you, to make you see them as I do, so clearly in my mind, nor to record to you their unique voices. How I wish tapes and videos had been known in those days, so that you could hear Sabine's bell-like singing voice, as we heard it in church on Sundays. His speaking voice was vibrant, a quality I never heard in any other. He did not speak much. One felt his mind was working all the time. When he did speak it was in quick perky sentences – always witty and interesting, and he loved to tease. But Grace, hers was the most beautiful speaking voice I have ever heard; like velvet – *mellow* is the word that best describes her. What a hard life she had. Transported from a simple background to being the Squire's lady in a large house, and I believe when she first came to Lew she was exposed to some hostility from the snobbish gentry in the countryside around. Fourteen children to cope with, and the house in such disrepair that there were workmen in and out of the house all her life, doing one thing or another. Then there was her eccentric husband, so united to her in love, but he can't have been easy to live with and certainly he was of no practical help. She had plenty of reason to be crotchety at times, yet in all the years I knew her (and I saw a great deal of her) I never saw her flustered or out of temper. She was always the same – warm, interested and gently humorous. I just loved them both and was proud to be related to them.

Lew House was bustling with life in those days, full of activity, and Ardoch, where my Granny lived on top of the hill, always full throughout every summer. Granny piled us all in and poured love on us. Lew was my heaven and I was often there apart from in the summer holidays. When I felt a sore throat coming on, I would pray that it would develop into really bad flu, so that the doctor would say, "Better send her down to her Grandmother."

In those early years the whole atmosphere was so different. When one looks back it seems ridiculously snobbish – such a strict dividing line between the big houses and the cottages. For instance, when any of the women and girls met the ladies of the big houses, they dropped a little curtsey. It was just the way things were, and it was all taken for granted. I suppose there was a sort of dignity about it all and there was a lot of love and caring. Granny and Aunt Alice were always concerned if anyone was ill or in trouble and did all they could to help. Of course there was no transport in the village except at Lew House and Ardoch, with their carriages, so if anyone had to go to hospital one or other would harness up and take them, returning for them when they were ready for home. Uncle Sabine was always aware of his flock and his daily outings, when he set forth in the dog-cart every morning after breakfast. This was the time he went to visit anyone he wanted to speak to or to enquire after anyone sick. I always remember a day when I met a woman whose husband I knew was ill. I enquired after him and she said, "Oh, me dear, Squire, he put us in a tizzy 'smorning. He come in and up the stairs to the bedroom 'fore us was vitty." This was typical of him. A sudden impulse. Passing the cottage, he remembered that one of his own was ill, so of course he must pop in to see how things were. It would not occur to him that it might be inconvenient. If he had no other business on these early-morning trips, he would call in at Ardoch as we were still breakfasting. He would say something outrageous to Granny. His stepmother was only a few years older than himself and he loved to tease her and she enjoyed his fun. She would answer "Naughty boy, hokus pokus!" There was a lovely relationship between them.

One wonderful day he appeared while we were still breakfasting. "Morning Granny, Joan's here. Got her motor car. Going to Dartmoor. Want to take Irene." I was thrilled. I don't remember how old I was at the time, but I know I had never been for a ride in a car, so it was as if a child today were offered a trip to the moon! Permission was given and I was soon installed on the edge of the back seat by Joan, very shy but bursting with excitement. Uncle Sabine in the front with the chauffeur and everyone in the house out to speed us on our way. As we drove to the moors, people popped out of their houses to gape at the fabulous horseless carriage.

Sometimes when I look back at it all, I wonder if I really lived it, or did I perhaps just read it in a book?

LEW CHURCH

Since there are now so few people — and soon there will be no-one — who remembers Lew Church as it was in the old days, I must put on record my memories of how it was in the early part of the century.

A few years ago I visited the church for the Sunday morning service, and felt very sad. There were just seven people there – the Rector and his daughter, the organist, we three visitors and one other. What a contrast from the days of my childhood, when the church on a Sunday morning would be quite full. All of us in our Sunday best – Granny and Aunt Grace still dressed in the way of Victorian ladies, voluminous black clothes and little black bonnets atop. What would they think of us now – even nonagenarians garbed like anyone else!

On Sunday mornings, Granny arrived in state in her brougham, driven by Tom Lang, her gardener-coachman, and drawn by fat old Ruby, who looked far more at home harnessed to the cart and setting forth to fetch coal for the house from Coryton station. In summer time, this equipage was full. Granny, in her abounding hospitality, filled the house to capacity all through the summer. Those for whom there was no room scrambled down Ragged Lane, which in far earlier times had been the main coach road into Cornwall.

How things have changed. Though not really so long ago, the snobbishness of those days is almost impossible to believe; yet, at the time, we took it all in our stride and as the normal and proper way to live!

So, the way we sat in church was very strictly adhered to. In the front seat centre sat Lew House – any overflow having to retire to the pews on the left. Row two was reserved for Mr and Mrs Sperling. They sat in solitary state as they had no children and I never remember seeing any visitors with them. Row three was cut in half by a pillar and the two seats beside it were for Granny. There was always competition between us as to who should have the privilege of sitting beside her, the others having to use the pews on the left. Next in status was Mrs Arundle and young Roger, the Curate's wife and son and seat five was for the schoolmaster and his family, the Dawes. After this came the hoi polloi.

The righthand pews followed the same pattern. They were for the servants of the big houses. So, of course the first two housed the Lew House lot. Then the Spurlings, and in the fourth Florrie usually sat alone, Selina being in the choir up near the organ. Lang, when Dora and I tried to persuade him to sit in what we considered his rightful place, invariably answered: "Well, Missie, I don't reckon I be any better than anybody else in this here village, so I sits at the back to make sure!" What an old darling he was. We haven't finished yet. The very important members of the community — the farmers. Their place was sideways on to the sanctuary.

The sermon was the highlight of the service, especially when Uncle Sabine preached. It was never longer than five minutes, and always very pithy. The other remarkable part of the service was the singing of the psalms. These were sung verse by verse in turn by Uncle Sabine in his lovely tenor voice and the coarse Devon voices of the choir topped by the unmusical and strident Selina. What a pity all this happened before the days of tapes or records, so the memory of it all is lost.

After the service came the parliament. We all foregathered outside for a good "Tell" as they say in Devon. This was eventually broken up when Lang reappeared with the equipage to transport us back to Ardoch and the huge Sunday lunch. How we ate in those days!

✧✧✧✧✧✧✧✧

THE HEIRS SINCE 1924

With the end of the Great War, punitive inheritance taxes were introduced. All sorts of methods and ways and means were sought to avoid the full impact.

Sabine before his death willed his estate to his son Edward. He claims that it was because they thought him incompetent to run it, as he was then in his 89th year. He became quite bitter and querulous, forgetting that his policy during his life had been to exclude his eldest son from any participation in the estate.

Most of Sabine's sons left England; Edward himself created a dynasty in America. After the 1914-18 War, when Edward was sent back from the trenches in poor health, he returned to Lew to discover that all was not well with the tax situation. His father was failing and he himself had not been encouraged to take much interest in the estate.

The real reason for the transfer of the estate from Sabine to Edward was in effect to protect the property. His lack of preparedness had created the very real danger of having the whole place broken up by death duty taxes. The full story is a closed book, except that it altered the normal inheritance and affected Edward's son Sabine Linton Baring-

Edward

Gould, who was then living and working in America. He was the father of the present owner, Merriol, and the titular owner from about 1956 to 1972. This was a short period and a frustrating inheritance. By the time he did come into the estate, he had made his way in America very successfully. He was the first expert on radar and was actively involved in the Second World War.

Sabine Linton

As part of this arrangement, the estate was managed by Trustees, through whose "mangling hands" every wish, of Sabine Linton's was ignored. He was kept in the dark about any plans for the old family home, and to make matters worse, one of the Trustees was his stepmother. This was a singularly tactless selection which lacked understanding.

The house at Lew was his in name, but in no way his to control – a cruel blow of fate, ensuring that he paid the price for his grandfather's original bad decision. If Edward had not been kept as far from the estate as possible in the early days, he may not have become an American citizen and everything would have been much easier.

The throbbing heart of the estate was dependant on the farms, the land, forests and mill to make it self-supporting. It comprised a small community in its own right, sustaining a large labour force. The needs of the estate gave work and prosperity and a way of life to a substantial group of people. Some who had lived in the location for generations felt that their lives were woven into and interdependent on the welfare and prosperity of the Squire.

Unfortunately, this way of life has been disrupted, and due to progressive taxes, more and more land has been sold. The more saleable farms and cottages have been sold in preference to the big old house, so, after a succession of blows, the Old Heart of the property had lost most of its working assets, which had kept it thriving in a health financial state, and in good maintenance and repair. The poor old house was like a man with both arms and legs amputated, left to flounder through relentless time, shorn of all its assets and totally unable to support itself any more.

Finally this dismembered body had to be leased to anyone brave enough to try to control and develop it in a different form. It was at that time deprived of enough self-generating income to keep it going in its old state. It began its journey, from 1931 as a tenanted house.

Edward's grand-daughter, the present owner and titular head of the property, the eldest daughter of Sabine Linton and his first wife Constance, lives in America with her husband Dr Douglas Almond MD. They have four children, Catherine, Christopher, Elizabeth (Betsy) and Douglas Jnr. Her sister Constance has two children and also lives in the States.

Merriol Baring-Gould Almond

Dr Merriol Baring-Gould Almond, on her father's death, inherited the estate. It came as a great shock to her, as her father had not warned her of this possibility. She walked into a terrible administrative mess. I will quote Merriol's letter, which is self-explanatory:-

> *Merriol Almond inherited Lew Trenchard when her father Sabine Linton died in Boston in 1972. Technically, in 1962 Merriol inherited Lew from her grandfather Edward. This was to save inheritance tax; Sabine's generation was skipped over, control resting during Sabine's lifetime in the hands of trustees. Sabine was reticent about Lew with Merriol, frustrated by the powerless position he had been placed in and his lack of current information. Sabine visited Lew infrequently, finding the changes since he grew up there painful and repugnant. therefore Merriol learned little from her father and had visited Lew with her father only for the christening in 1971 of her elder son Christopher Sabine.*

Since Merriol did not want to sell Lew or uproot herself and her family, absentee ownership has continued. She has tried to be as well informed and as closely involved in Lew Trenchard, which she has done with great dedication and careful attention to detail. In 1990 she established the Baring-Gould Corporation.

Technically, she is still the owner, but this new arrangement, which was set up with the expert advice of her cousin John Raboul, an American lawyer well versed in English and American law, developed the Corporation. It appears to be a convoluted method of overcoming the problems of her being an American citizen and her potential heirs being put in a similar position. Merriol is Director of the Baring-Gould Corporation. Douglas Snr, Catherine, Elizabeth, Christopher and young Doug are officers. They all obviously know exactly the position of the property, with all the complex machinations of American and English law. As none of them wants to sell the property, they have had to find a way of safeguarding the next heir, who incidentally will not be chosen until such time as the four candidates have decided which way their respective lives with go professionally.

As stated before, they have in turn throughout their lives accompanied their mother on her regular visits to her English inheritance. They, unlike their mother, have had ample time and opportunity to think deeply on this situation which they have all inherited. We have all met the four and Douglas Snr, so we are united in the problems and know the heirs as individuals, which is as it should be. I am sure that Sabine is sighing with a deep sense of relief that Merriol has sorted out this mess that she inherited, with such aptitude and ability.

I may be a bit "way out", but I feel that now Sabine can move on his way and get on with his new destiny, as the mistakes he unconsciously made have been rectified, chiefly by Merriol, but perhaps in part by all of us who came along to clear up some of the mess.

She found to her dismay that the estate had been grossly mismanaged. The agents had been left almost totally alone to run the establishment. Much had been stolen and/or mislaid. The priceless furniture was in an appalling condition, the books, the pride and joy of Sabine's life, were rotting on shelves, sodden from the leaks. The Trustees were perhaps unable to find the cash or the solutions to the problems. During that period of history, there were many changes in the life of this country, with altering standards at every level. There was also another War looming, which distracted attention from the needs of a cumbersome old building.

Bickford Dickinson, when he was the incumbent, found he could not stay at Lew. As the representative of the family through his mother, Mary (Sabine and Grace's eldest child), he felt ashamed. He was totally frustrated by the current situation in the estate management. The escalating complaints from tenants were all directed at him, which was embarrassing when he was also the local Vicar. He retired after a short period. This really saddened him, as he had hoped to continue to hold the job as his grandfather would no doubt have liked, until natural retirement age. Bickford knew and respected Sabine, and had a deep love for his mother. He doubly wanted to be in her homeland and her church.

Grandfather Sabine did not think out the future, and thus brought about the present American-owned Corporation. I am sure Merriol will forgive me if I say that her great-grandfather must now see that America has come to save the day.

With the help of tenants since 1950, the house has gradually pulled itself out of the terrible malaise it had fallen into. Merriol has been able to keep her finger on the pulse, with the great support of her husband.

This story could apply to many similar Manor Houses, but this one is an "epic" of survival. Sabine Baring-Gould turned it into a most unique and attractive small country house, set in serene surroundings, a place of great interest to people from far and wide. He achieved his objective, but only just...In the nick of time it was saved by the many who have taken pity on the house, and by the timely arrival of a vigorous caring Squire(ess). Everything is due to Merriol, for her energy and the application she has given to her inheritance.

She has been fortunate, since she inherited the house, to have had caring tenants, who have developed and created a magnificent and renowned hotel and restaurant. It is currently being very ably managed by the Murrays. All the recent tenants, including the Paynters and Jim Purdy have contributed to the Soul of the House.

Postscript: To those who were not heirs, yet had the right to call this house "Home", this is a Dedication. All those sons and daughters who have or have not been mentioned in these pages, who started their lives here and contributed their personalities and energies into making it what it is today. To those who have wandered away to all corners of the earth, they have been remembered by the house. The word "Lew" can mean *to make warm* or *to shelter from the wind.* The word "Lew" means a lot to many people.

Beloved place, we thank you for your gift of just being where you are and what you are.

The TOAST 1979

On June 18th 1979 an interesting event took place. A dinner party grew quite spontaneously out of a gathering of descendants of the family, some of whom had never been to the house before.

Michael Baring-Gould, who lived in Anchorage, Alaska, with his wife Wendy and three children Laura, Ian and Jonathan, had previously arranged a trip over to England during the summer holidays, and naturally had planned a visit to Devonshire and to Lew Trenchard. On the spur of the moment, prior to flying, they all decided that a visit to Michael's father's (Teddy Baring-Gould) home would not be complete without Teddy. They telephoned him in California and persuaded him to travel to England at the same time. Teddy is very flexible and readily agreed. The three generations met at Lew Trenchard having flown in from California and Alaska respectively. It was an exciting moment.

In the meantime Connie Baring-Gould Merriot had arranged to travel to Scotland to join a musical seminar at roughly the same time. She had arranged with her sister Merriol Baring-Gould Almond for the two of them to visit Lew Trenchard together. Merriol changed the date of her visit to fit in with the idea. She brought her daughter Betsy over with her. Thus the three of them were at Lew Trenchard at the same time as Teddy, Michael and family. All these arrangements grew spontaneously and quite separately from each other. Merriol and Connie are Teddy's nieces and although they all live in the States, live so far apart that they rarely meet. In fact it was the first time these three cousins had met together, and it happened to be at Lew Trenchard.

Quite obviously other local members of our family foregathered to meet up with the relatives from the States. There were seventeen of us present that night of June 18th: the Calmady Hamlyn family – Warwick, Joan and Angela; Eulalia Newman (Rowe); Madge Dickinson; three Briggs and Lorna Mattocks (née Baring-Gould). Lorna walked in unknowing that a far flung family gathering had assembled. Strangely, she had not visited the old house for years and had felt prompted to do so that week.

It was a momentous evening, culminating with the four younger members getting up and making a remarkable toast, which was totally spontaneous. There was a great deal of jumping about as they apparently all wanted to be spokesman!

"Let us stand and drink a toast to our past ancestors and to those present here for making this meeting possible in this old house."

We all solemnly raised our glasses and drank to our mutual heritage. It brought tears to the eyes of the more senior members. The age of the four youngsters ranged from 9-12 years. Suddenly those of us immediately involved in the present day struggle to survive realised that it REALLY was worth all the effort required to keep the old "flag" of the Baring-Goulds flying — and that the "jewel" in the centre of the Estate WAS worth all the blood, sweat and tears required to keep it resplendent. There is ALWAYS another generation to follow who will be proud of their heritage and play their part continuing the saga.

Following upon that June meeting another contingent of Baring-Goulds arrived from Rhodesia: June, Dawn and Sabine. They had previously arranged a meeting with Teddy and his wife Barbara at Lew Trenchard.

Sunday May 26th 1991
The Gathering at Lew Trenchard was an exciting and successful occasion for all who came. It seemed that all, from the youngest to the oldest, were making this a great family event. So many had not met before, and others hadn't seen each other for a long time.

Altogether, there were 119 of us, including the family support groups of locals, the PCC and members of the Sabine Baring-Gould Appreciation Society. There were 98 for the church service.

There was not one Baring-Gould present, though sixty-six of us could claim to be descended from that name. There were over twenty from Arthur Baring-Gould's side, headed by Irene Widdecombe, who, at well over ninety, is mentally as sprightly as ever. Bless her for coming.

With the amazing generosity of everyone, donations from the beginning of the year total £1,420; the church collection was £129; the picnic raised £550 - all this contributes to one great onslaught against the death watch beetle. More has to be collected, of course, to complete the job, but the screen is safe for some time, having been very well repaired. The Parish Church Council do thank you all for your enormous support.

None of us will forget the fun that we all had. The wonderful sunshine, the folk singing by John Hobbs, the first strawberries of the season with clotted cream, and the trip around the house. A day to remember.

By the way, on May 26th 1872, Sabine came into the Estate. His father Edward died on that day, 119 years ago, and there were 119 souls supporting this gathering! A strange coincidence of numbers, one for the numerologists. Perhaps it was a planned event and not a coincidence.

THE TENANTS

The Paynters and the Purdys

Around 1950, the Paynters came with a small Scots friend called Jim Purdy to look at Lew House. They were shocked to see the sad state of the house. It was in a derelict state, the gardens thoroughly overgrown.

They felt that they HAD to rescue the place. A quixotic gesture, they had not counted the cost of energy and finance. It is known that Mrs Paynter, with her womanly eyes, could see at a glance what this was to entail in blood, sweat and tears. However, the men decided that it was worth a try to get to grips with the deterioration. They managed to get a low rental with a part repairing tenancy. The cleaning of the interior alone was a massive task. The local women were so sorry for Mrs P. that a number came along and helped her with some of these terrific chores necessary to reach a state of relative cleanliness.

It proved to be a huge undertaking for all, inside and out. Everywhere there was dirt, the accumulation of the work of countless spiders festooned so thickly layer upon layer, covering everything along the way – walls and all nooks and crannies. It was so thick and dense that the pictures still miraculously hanging on the walls were so hidden that their appearance was a surprise to those working in the area.

Water had been dripping for years in the back library onto a collection of some of Sabine's assortment of books. Many had to be thrown away.

Prior to the Paynters seeing the house, it had been empty for a while. Before this, two spinster sisters had tenanted the house. They had been recommended by the Bishop of Exeter. The poor man could not have known them very well, as they had two secret addictions: they loved their drink and they collected dogs.

The wretched dogs were prisoners in the courtyard and were never let out from that area at the back of the house, which incidentally opened onto the kitchens. So bad was the stench that tradesmen refused to deliver.

Later on the Paynters were clearing the rose garden of overgrown debris when they found a huge cache of empty bottles, which gave the sisters' secret away. It took two or three lorry loads to remove this memento of their stay.

There were rats once again resident in the roof over the gallery. (When we took over the tenancy the rat colony had returned and set up such a huge metropolis that it took two lorry loads to remove their homes.) Evidently the rats think it as much their home as we do. So do the bats.

Jim the Scotsman was not married at that time and he nobly worked all hours to get the house into a liveable state. He appeared to be a "Jack of all Trades". He went to work at one of the local factories to help out with the finances. Eventually they all had to think of ways and means of making the house pay its way, to subsidise the enormous cost of repairs, heating and light bills. There were so many broken panes of glass, they lost count. The lead was so soft and cracked that it desperately needed replacing.

There were only two workable baths, but the hot water supply was hopelessly unreliable. The boiler was underground in the courtyard and had a nasty habit of becoming flooded after any heavy rain. Out would go the boilers, resulting in a total stoppage of heat and hot water. The sewage system was nonexistent, spewing across fields, and had been in this state for some years by the look of the ground in the area.

In due course the Paynters decided to turn the house into a guest house with a restaurant. It then grew gradually into something bigger and better. Eventually they were able to use most of the rooms and the House became popular for functions such as weddings and special events. It is a strange phenomenon – the people who have used the house have a very protective paternal attitude towards its welfare. They become in some obscure way identified with its atmosphere.

Mrs Paynter's speciality was her Sunday teas. Delicious cream teas with all homemade scones and cakes and wonderful sweets. One in particular was known as Heavenly Pie. Lew House became very popular for Sunday outings, drawing people from Plymouth in particular. the teas, including cakes, cost the princely sum of 2/6d per head! They had as many as 200 people over at the height of their fame. This was up to about 1965. But their prices and the rising costs never kept up with the insatiable demands of the house for repairs of one kind or another.

Alan Paynter had great charisma as a host. His mother, whose cooking was of the delicious homemade variety, was a very hard-working lady. I believe his father cherished the gardens, returning them to a semblance of order.

Jim had married by this time and he and his wife toiled as hard as the Paynters to try to make the place pay its way. Jim became famous with the guests. He was much loved and much sought after. He seemed able to recognise people which made him very popular. They came back again and again, always asking for Jim. He became the head waiter and main factotum and was indispensible. We in our turn found him so. He stayed on with us when the Paynters sold the lease to us in 1975. They were worn out by then with the struggle and constant pressure of numbers and the many events during the year. When they came to sell the tenancy, I feel sure it was the daunting thought of having to satisfy the fire regulations with all kinds of new installations.. Also there was the whole of the electric wiring to be renewed. It had been there for about thirty years and was hopelessly out of date and lethally inadequate for the new phase of the house's life.

The Paynters had saved the house for another phase of its life. The Baring-Goulds owe them a debt of great gratitude for their contribution to the house at a very low moment of its life. To see the house today it would be hard to imagine the state it was in when the Paynters took over. They developed its potential, turning it into a well-known establishment.

"We" then stepped in to take on this load of worry, as the next set of unsuspecting tenants. The date was October 18th 1975.

Since 1975

"We" represented my daughter Sallie; my husband; myself; a great friend called Robert Lambert who was an able plumber/electrician and odd job man; and the two Brooks, John and Anne, who were related to my husband. John had worked for some time in Hotel management and so knew the ropes. We seemed to be an energetic group, well covered (we thought) for the future of the house.

Sallie is most capable with her hands. The furnishings were incredibly shabby and she took on the mammoth task of replacing curtains, chair covers, bed covers and miles of carpet. She sewed all by herself on a tiny little sewing machine. Also, she later took over the full charge of all the catering, when John and Anne left us. (There was insufficient money to support us all, and they had two children.) I filled in the gaps and became the front woman, and the breakfast woman when we had residents. My husband nobly took on the accounts and the bookkeeping, which he loathed.

We had decided to make it a hotel rather than a restaurant, but there were insufficient bedrooms to make it profitable, so we had to keep the restaurants continuing as they had been. Sometimes there were three dining rooms in action at the same time. Not an ideal situation, as the dining rooms interfered with the bedrooms. The house was not soundproofed and was not designed as a function venue. Far too many people used the place at one time. The Long Room contained over forty covers and had a dance floor with a band. In its heyday it operated for three days a week. Somehow we managed, although we worried about the stability of the dance floor. It required an RSJ to support it.

We employed two wonderful chefs and they helped to raise our catering standards. We began to win awards with their expertise, and slowly moved into a different type of clientele. We had hoped to ultimately cut down on the numbers for catering, and on the numbers using the house. We felt it was detrimental to its welfare to have so many. The present tenants have found the right balance to preserve the fabric of the house.

In addition to the expense, we had had many setbacks which others had not experienced. The weather had taken us to the wall on so many occasions, we felt bedevilled by it. The first year, 1976, we ran into the worst drought in recent times, when all the water in our reservoir (a private one supplying two farms and ourselves) completely ran dry. We had to buy water daily, with all the attendant headaches of insufficient bathwater for guests and huge washing-up problems. It was a nightmare time.

Over New Year 1976-7 there was a terrific storm, and about twenty trees came down. The roads were blocked and all the telephone lines out of action. Our New Year's Eve food had to be eaten up by a handful of us for several days.

Then on February 16th a blizzard hit us. It was so sudden that Jim, who lived only ten minutes away, hardly got home. Snow was several feet deep in minutes. The sky was pitch black and again the telephone lines came down, along with the electric cables. We had to keep warm with one very badly smoking fire in the front hall. Fortunately we had a gas cooker, so managed to cook. As a precaution against the water freezing in the roof, we turned the water off and resorted to manually carrying it everywhere. We were terrified that the pipes would burst and bring the ceilings down.

That wasn't the end of it. The following winter we had rain and more rain. So much that the stream at the back flooded. We placed sandbags across the courtyard gates to prevent water entering the house. Teddy had warned us that the house could flood. We were beaten by the road at the back becoming a lake. The water built up and started to pour through the back walls of the Long Room. We just had to keep on sweeping water away for hours until it all subsided. We had to co-opt the help of our resident guests, who all nobly rolled up their trousers and swept and swept to keep the terrible flood from entering the house. With their help we succeeded, but we were all exhausted. It was an amazing sight, to see a lake where the lower rose garden had been. I wished I had a camera to record the event. It soon disappeared down to the Quarry. (At some time in the history of the garden construction, the flow of the stream had been deflected. On these angry occasions, streams do not like having their natural courses interfered with. It certainly was angry that day.) That was January 1979.

The final piece of sabotage was wrought by fire. A huge chunk of burning tarring disgorged itself after we had had the chimney swept in the main hall, and crashed down onto the parquet flooring, with its highly polished surface. Instantly the flames were licking up the wonderful "overmantel" and starting to fill the room with thick acrid smoke. It was suffocating.

Sallie and Robert were on the spot fast, and with great presence of mind they pulled the carpet over the flames and smothered the fire, with the help of furnishings and fire extinguishers. By the time the fire engines arrived (in a remarkably short time) from Tavistock, these two had controlled what could have been a very real disaster.

It seemed to us that we experienced the wrath of the four elements, so perhaps, as it had been within our tenancy as representative of the family, we had made amends for any past neglect by a variety of our forebears. We certainly had to pay through our teeth for the experience. It was interesting and very challenging and most of the time we enjoyed the opportunity to learn. We did our best to bring it up a step further. It was now an acknowledged Hotel and the food was in a classified category.

We had replaced an enormous amount of the essentials to keep the house reasonably clean, watertight and firesafe, and so many other little things needed to upgrade it. We completed the fireproofing, the water pipes replaced in many places, the new sewage system, the RSJ in the Long Room, the flooring in the front hall, endless basins in bedrooms and some bathrooms added. Plus decoration, external and internal.

We left the house wiser, and I have to admit very relieved to be away from the endless strain of the "unexpected". We had been hit below the belt so many times, it all became too much. We ran out of money – as simple as that!

On January 18th 1980, we closed the hotel and had to say goodbye to all the wonderful staff who had stood by us through thick and thin. It was a sad moment. Merriol repurchased the remaining lease from us so that she could release it, as and when she wanted, giving her the right to control the next tenancy. For a short time it was opened to the public, but that did not provide enough revenue. She leased it to the Slades.

It is wonderful to see how succeeding tenants have all continued to contribute. We have all in our time, piece by piece, improved the place to keep "the Spirit of the House" alive. Sabine used to refer to this overshadowing form as "the Angel of the House". Whoever or whatever it is, it certainly takes its toll of those who own it and those who tenant it. It most certainly looks after itself.

Afer we left, the Slades took over for about three years. They added a lot of paint and carpeting. But Jennie was not well, and they sold to Marie Ellen and Greg, two enthusiastic Americans. They, however, were unable to stay long, due to some problems with work permits. In the short time they were in the house, they contributed a great deal to its elegance. They were also very adept at marketing and they literally promoted Lew Trenchard in the finest advertising papers in the States, including *The Manor House Hotels*, which had been a great catch and success. They employed a first-class chef who won awards for the quality of the food he produced.

They sold the lease to the present tenants – the Murrays. This year of 1993 sees them as tenants for five years. They have put in many touches of elegance with some beautiful drapes and elegant bedrooms. The bar looks lovely, the whole house gleams with polish and seems to be smiling contentedly, or purring like a well-fed cat! Even the gardens have had a tremendous uplift. They have maintained the quality and standard of the restaurant and won many awards and rosettes.

Long may they stay and continue with this fine standard of hospitality. The Murrays are both caring and clever and very welcoming to those of us who return at intervals, particularly the enormous brood of the endless offshoots of the Baring-Gould tribe. Let us hope that "The Spirit of the House" will protect and cherish them for as long as they want to stay.

The house MUST be at peace now. So much love and energy has gone into "the" welfare, to keep all the powerful "energy lines" flowing in a "Godly way", in peace and harmony.

LEW HOUSE 1086 – 1993

Cicely Baring-Gould

Our "Miss Cicely", as she was fondly referred to – my mother – was the thirteenth child; and was sufficiently far down the line of Baring-Gould children that she hardly knew her parents. She was sent away to bearding school in Launceston at the tender age of five, and then afflicted with a series of harsh holiday governesses who were instructed to cram some semblance of learning into the minds of the younger Baring-Gould children. From all accounts they were not a promising bunch of students, considered to be wild, unruly and unresponsive, their lives a paradox of extremes. They were very strictly controlled by governesses, ignored by their father, and their mother too tired and ill to have the opportunity to know them. Yet almost from the momenht they could walk they were expected to ride – and ride they did at every opportunity. My mother was a fine horsewoman as were many of her brothers and sisters. She rode sidesaddle and I can remember seeing the flowing grace of horse and rider – they became one. She had a magic touch with her hands, animals seemed to respond to some magnetic quality that flowed from her. Later on she used to walk into the animal-strewn jungles of India, totally unafraid.

She was the last of the Baring-Gould girls to marry. She stayed and nursed her sick mother until Grace died in 1916, and then she managed the house for her father until her marriage to her handsome cavalry officer in 1917. They had two days' honeymoon, after which she returned to Lew until 1919. She then left for India to join her husband – from that time she rarely visited her old home, and after 1931, when the house ceased to be the family home, she would not return. She had her reasons. The memories of the home she knew, the gardens and stables as remembered in the days when her large family lived in the house, she wanted to keep unchanged. To the end of her days she remained a "Devonshire Maid", her heart buried deep in the house of her forebears. No other country, or county for that matter, to her way of thinking, ever measured up to the unique quality of her beloved Devon and the freedom of Dartmoor, which she knew so well from the days of her riding youth.

Although her childhood was spent in idyllic surroundings, the way of life was harsh and impoverished. I remember her telling me that the first new dress she ever owned was the one her bridegroom bought her for her wedding day in 1917. Up to then she had had clothes cut down to fit and shoes passed on from sister to sister. She had an allowance of fifty pounds a year from her father's estate after his death, so that she did not have to be totally dependent upon her husband for her every need. This pittance of independence was shortlived. Her life was not one of material riches, but a heritage of

Cicely Newport Tinley

interest. She had lived in an epoch of history which died with the Great War. She saw the end of an era for the lives of those who were part of the manorial life in rural England, and she herself had to change, and change fast – emotionally she had taken on a tough assignment. Life married to an army officer meant constant separations, either from her husband or from her children, who were sent to England to school. A great heartache for one with a soft heart! She had few of the joys of seeing her children grow up; only a few snatched months every three years and then back to India. A lifetime of many farewells, and then to lose her only son at the age of nineteen in 1940. He was shot down in flames over Holland. Bitter sweet memories! Despite all this, she had her mother's puckish sense of humour and was a wicked "tease" as her father had been before her. She had learnt to adapt!

This book is to her memory and the memory of the three handsome men in her life.
I dedicate this booklet to them – to keep their lives evergreen in the days to come.

Col. Frank Newport Tinley

Gervase Newport Tinley

Simon Charles Briggs

ENERGY FIELDS - A Basic Understanding

Leylines. The term used to express the earth's grid system. These are energy lines reputed to thread their way over the face of the earth, fine and unseen. For those of us who may not have clairvoyant vision, it is hard to accept. But so persistent are the claims, and so many have been the confirmations of sightings and locations. (Clairvoyant vision is capable of seeing through ultraviolet. This is a kind of dowsing, similar to dowsing for water.)

There is a general consensus that these energy lines have junction points or confluences. At these points, where several energies meet, a building is to be found to act as a resonator or echo container. Sound was the vital factor.

These energies need stimulating, or recharging, frequently. Water movement appears to assist in resonating these soundwaves in the required manner. There are many ancient "holy" wells attached to churches. This is an ideal way to co-opt mankind (unconsciously) into activating these sound waves by singing hymns, anthems, chanting, etc. By creating churches, cathedrals and other places of worship, the loud songs of praise were further encouraged by a powerful organ, which increased the volume of sound. Curved ceilings added to the resonance. In this way, we are maintaining the unseen flows of these hidden forces.

Thus the minds of men were impressed through intuitive perception. Our minds were impressed to build some of these magnificent houses to the Glory of God. Some majestic places fulfil this double function.

Some time in the future we will all know more. In the past it was necessary to use subterfuge to protect these precious energies. Now we have to be aware, look and listen, be tolerant of that which we do not understand or have the perception to see ourselves and play our part in the developing process of rediscovering these patterns of the past.

In the case of Lew Trenchard Church, it was Sabine who really began the development and beautification of this church and the house, for the benefit of posterity. He put a great deal of effort and energy into preserving it after years of almost total neglect.

He has left behind various symbols and indications of his own inner awareness of the importance of the deeper aspects of his place in the scheme of things. He achieved his objective, as we have seen through much of this booklet. He has redeemed much of the negative magnetic impulses spilt over the area in warfare, feuds and hatreds. His old home will survive. It is filled with age-old works of creation...